# *Of* VALENTINES *and* VISIONS

# CAMILLE DUPLESSIS

*N. still doesn't seem tired of these! How lucky am I? Thank you, too, for deciding there's nowhere better.*

Here we are with the second half of the arc set after *The Kraken and The Canary,* but before *Like Silk Breathing.* I finished this up during a particularly hectic time in my personal life, and world events also reaffirmed my desire to create gothic-flavored romance where queer people—including those who aren't nice—aren't sacrificed upon an altar of morality. In this, Bertie is a little like David in *Like Silk Breathing* and *The Only Story,* although maybe more directly impacted by his insistence upon keeping his abilities and traumas secret.

There are almost always hard themes present in this series, so it feels difficult to list everything that could be triggering, such as bereavement, alcohol misuse, suicide attempts, and so on. (If I've neglected to be clear about a trigger beforehand, it isn't to be callous or provocative. If you feel comfortable, let me know.) For transparency's sake: Bertie was neglected and abused as a child, as was Lucas.

None of it is really portrayed on the page, with the exception of brief descriptions or allusions, and of course, the poor crows from *Of Flint and Fortune*. I did toy with adding a specific content warning for them, but decided the whole idea was pretty evident from the blurb, and nothing was graphically described…and it may be amusing for readers to know that I've been vegan for over ten years. Before then, I went vegetarian as a kid. (I cried *a lot* about veal, bacon, and lamb.)

Naturally, explanations are not justifications or excuses; characters and circumstances in Threads of Wyrd are meant to be somewhat unsettling and often dark, and not quite what they seem. At the same time, earnestness and whimsy are equally important to me. And an interesting historical note for one of my settings that applies to *Valentines, Flint,* and *Kraken*: St Peter and St Paul was derelict in the early 1870s. It had been in decline well before then. The efforts to repair the tower and nave, and rebuild the chancel, culminated in the 1880s.

I hope you enjoy exploring this world as much as I've loved crafting it.

**1**

———

EDINBURGH—OCTOBER 1849

The boy who delivered his parents' order from the butcher had red hair and thin arms that should have struggled carrying the box, but didn't. He toddled a bit, given the uneven path beneath his feet, but that was all. Clearly, Bertie Calder thought, as he watched from between some thick leaves, he was from the *lower orders*. His parents called them that, anyway, although he wasn't entirely sure what they meant by it.

Father was a physician in demand with the richer set and Mother's family was distantly related to the royal family, although her branch had lost its titles and connections sometime in the century before. However they meant it, they did not mean well. Father said he believed in God and Jesus, but any mercy afforded by either did not seem to extend to the poor.

Given the boy's visibly mended clothes and smudged face, he was not from New Town or any of the worlds its residents frequented. Bertie leaned forward slightly and tried to get a better view without exposing his position. He had never been allowed to really speak with anyone his mother or father deemed unsuitable. It was not the done thing, of course, and he had few opportunities to subvert it of his own accord. Even servants were not to be interacted with, which Bertie did not understand.

Mrs. Yardley, the housekeeper here in Edinburgh, was kind. And the caretaker at the house near Cromer had once showed him a gaggle of new kittens born close to the old duckpond, and the butler in London was prone to slipping him a sweet every now and again. Sweets weren't permitted. Neither were kittens. But Mr. Carlyle, the caretaker, had taken them home after it was made known that no kittens were allowed in the Calders' house or even any outbuildings.

Bertie crept closer to the red-headed boy, fairly confident that their modest garden's foliage shielded him from notice. The redhead was near the servants' door on the side of the house, waiting to be relieved of his errand, balancing the box with expert ability. He seemed bored, if anything, and Bertie wanted to know why in the world someone with an occupation would be bored.

"I can hear you," said the boy, without looking in Bertie's direction. "These houses don't have big gardens. Can't be sneaking anywhere if you don't know how to in the first place, anyway."

Immediately, Bertie was both incensed and intrigued. The boy's speech marked him as being from the city, if not New Town itself. Or as far as Bertie knew, it did. He hadn't much experience with Edinburgh just yet, and he could not say he liked it on such short acquaintance. Most of all, he liked Norfolk, which Father worked very hard to seem as though he was not from, and Bertie supposed London was all right enough.

Reluctant to admit the boy had noticed him at all, but knowing that to pretend he wasn't there was silly, Bertie sighed and stepped onto the path. Summoning all the dignity he was supposed to have, he said, "I'm Albert Calder. I like your shoes." Unlike the rest of the boy's clothes, his shoes were obviously new and well cared for, or they were so new, they had not yet become dirty and worn.

*At least he has shoes.* Some of the more luckless youngsters did not, or so he was sometimes reminded if his parents decided he was being ungrateful for what he had; he never lacked shoes or anything he needed.

"Your surname's on the order."

"I should hope so," said Bertie, "as my father employs the housekeeper who made it."

"Old Mrs. Reid," the boy said. "She's all right."

"Mrs. Yardley," Bertie said. "Mrs. Reid is the cook."

What seemed like embarrassment, followed by a light flush of pink, passed over the boy's face. Then he wriggled his nose as though he wished to ease an itch. Bertie's eyes darted to his hands, which kept the box securely in place, held to his chest. This boy could not be any older than him, although it was difficult to tell when a person had such a pinched, starved air and held himself as though he was generally underfed. He was probably not as big as he should have been.

He could only assume this boy's age, although perhaps he was also just wishing for them to have something in common. At eleven, he still did not have many friends, though he was trying to be more sociable because everyone claimed it was a good, normal thing. "Who are you?"

"Me?"

"Yes, you. I don't see anybody else." Bertie did not say something that might indicate he thought his new house was haunted—though he almost did—or about how he often heard heavy footsteps along this side of it when no one at all was present. They usually happened at night, and he supposed, reading all the stories about highwaymen that he did, they might belong to burglars or awful people trying to see if the house was worth breaking into.

"Nobody, is who I am." The boy's nose scrunched again, and it was pinker now than it had been a moment ago. "Can't even get somebody to open this door, can I?"

Bertie considered it. Given all he'd been taught about how the Calders were meant to hold and comport themselves, he knew it would be beyond any possibility to let this box-bearing boy use the front door.

Though Bertie had just come out of it himself, that was one thing. This rather dirty young person could not go through it without creating a fuss. Michael was up from Cambridge, too, and in Bertie's experience, his elder brother was liable to create a scene when he was bored. Whenever he was up or down from Cambridge, he was bored. And that meant he was looking to cause trouble, some of which might involve pranks and in the worst cases, minor acts of violence against Bertie.

Speaking up didn't make a difference, for neither Mother nor Father believed anything was ever malicious upon Michael's part. All they knew about was the usual type of teasing and harassing, not that they listened if Bertie said he felt like it was too much.

They didn't know a thing about milky tea laced with

cannabis or various tinctures, some of which were readily available from any chemist or pilfered from Father's home stores. After the first couple of these cups of tea, which Bertie had consumed willingly, Michael had taken to capturing him in one arm and forcing them down his throat.

His parents also did not know about the enticing slices of cake, and biscuits, that Bertie would rather have not tasted at all. Or, perhaps worst of all, the weird little darts and needles dipped in nasty compounds that could make Bertie dizzy, or weak, or fall asleep quickly.

He was glad that, as a younger son, he was not necessarily expected to go to Cambridge. If all one learned there was how to poison people for fun, he didn't need the knowledge.

"Even nobodies have names," said Bertie. He pushed aside thoughts of university, knowing he might well have to go. Father might not care much about him now, but he wondered if, the older he got, the more likely it would be that expectations grew larger too. As a physician to the wealthy, Father did care about appearances. If he did need to go, perhaps he might study something like history or literature rather than ways of mildly poisoning people.

"The likes of you can't want mine."

"I shall thank you not to tell me what I want." Being told what he thought or wanted was a sore spot. Even if no one actually expected much of him, they certainly seemed to be able to tell him what he should want and how he should behave.

After a sigh that sounded more world weary than what Bertie imagined an old sailor's sigh to be, because he had not met any sailors even if he had read about them, the boy said, "I'm Will Lucas. Now, do you think a maid or someone will open this for me? I have other deliveries to make, or Old Ross will have my hide if I'm back after he says I should be."

Old Ross, that was the butcher. Mrs. Reid had mentioned him. She'd called him a radge and Bertie had never heard the word, if he had even heard it right given her accent. Her tone, and Mrs. Yardley's solemn agreement with the assessment, let him know it was not complimentary. He overheard them muttering later how Old Ross was temperamental and prone to outbursts, and supposed "radge" conveyed those qualities.

Then an awareness swept over him as they could: a clear picture of Will Lucas sitting on a bed in a dim, little room with angry bruises littered on his face, and somehow Bertie, in the way he often knew things that might happen, knew Ross would not be pleased no matter when Will returned. Bertie could not say how, he could never say how, but he knew this was Will in the near future. These visions usually happened while he slept, but weren't impossible during waking hours.

This would happen perhaps today, perhaps tomorrow. Soon. Unlike some of these scenes, this one felt absolutely true. "He will have it anyway, won't he?"

Will shrugged as though it did not matter, but his eyes said Bertie was right.

"Your room is narrow, more of a boxroom, and the bed has a blue quilt on it." He wondered who had made the quilt. A mother? Other mothers had to be better than his own, and he assumed they made things like quilts. "Why isn't he smart enough to bruise you *not* on your face?"

Mutely, Will just stared at him. Bertie decided Will must be a little sluggish.

Seized by the idea to do something good, Bertie said,

"Wait here." He dashed off, ignoring the halfhearted grumble following his ears, something like, *That's what I was doing*, and slipped inside without capturing Michael's attention, or anyone's. When he opened the side door for Will, the latter's expression was full of what looked to Bertie like disbelief over such a small gesture.

Proudly, he whispered, so as to continue his streak of passing undetected through the relatively small house, "Mind the parsnips on the table in the kitchen. But you can put the box there. Cook, Mrs. Reid, she will go through it."

Will preceded him to the hallway after Bertie stepped aside. Bertie was curious about this new delivery boy as he shut the door behind them. Although, he *was* moving as though he knew his way around. Maybe it was not his first time here, and only the first time Bertie had noticed him. He hoped it would not be the last.

By the time Will had gone on his way, Bertie was determined that he would have a new friend. They had not spoken inside the dark and quiet house, for that would have attracted attention he did not want, and he was reasonably confident nobody overheard them moving about. Unfortunately, that confidence proved to be misplaced, for his brother soon spoke from the shadows cast by the stairwell. Even in the limited daylight that their new home afforded, it seemed the house was forever breeding shadows.

"Bertie, if you were so lonely, you could have said. I have been dying to spend more time with my little brother."

Instinct said to back away, no, dash away, return to the garden where Michael wouldn't want to go because it was damp and gloomy outside, but Bertie knew he couldn't go fast enough with a wall at his back and Michael blocking his way forward. Bertie glanced at Michael's hand, where a little, yellow feather shone in the dim light.

He sighed.

In his experience, this particular shade of feather was always attached to a tiny dart, more of a needle, really. The needle would be coated with some drug that, once he'd been pricked, made Bertie feel warm, sleepy, and what he imagined adults felt when they were drunk. He hated the darts. Michael was studying in preparation to enter medicine, and he suspected his awful brother had gained new ideas and knowledge to torment him through this.

Certainly, he had been able to before, but not so creatively. The pranks and rough play had started innocently and tallied with what boys at school said about their siblings: shoelaces tied together, wrestling, mud in his seat. Once Michael left for university, though, they escalated to altered food or drink, and the mysterious feathered needles. He didn't know what happened to cause the change, but it was accompanied by a sharpish demeanor he did not recognize as belonging to the Michael he'd known before.

The drugs left no evidence, no marks or bruises or material traces of what had occurred. He was often rendered a little silly or slow or hazy under their influence. But it never coincided with a family meal, for instance, or any great length of time spent with their parents.

What good was being able to see the future if he never saw this before it was happening? More frozen than fearful, he edged away until his back met the wall. Michael was older than him, bigger than him, and faster than him. He might try to slip away, but somehow that always made things worse.

*Cromer—October 1872*

Will Lucas did not like leaving things unanswered. One day, he supposed it would get him into great trouble. Until it did, he planned on replying to everyone but God, whom he tended to give a wide berth on principle. As it seemed he was not blessed with a life he could be either proud of or happy with, it felt wise to keep himself away from any sort of divine notice.

As he chivvied open a first-floor window, he reckoned he would get answers out of Bertie Calder, one way or another. He'd even climbed up from the ground floor to get them. It hadn't been difficult because this old, stately house was the sort with enough external outcroppings for him to grab or use as footholds, and it was not a damp night.

To have been dragged into another's mess was not something he could easily forgive, and certainly not when the mess had to do with feelings. Bertie had too many romantic, or mad, ones for Alastair Gow.

Lucas had too many, too—but they were for Bertie. Which, on balance, was awful luck. Even as he made his way inside, he knew that even if he did not precisely forgive Bertie, Bertie would benefit from the softer feelings he possessed.

He fell to the floor with a nearly soundless drop, cushioned by an expensive Persian carpet. It was in some kind of little private library, the sort that only the wealthy would have, and easily navigable even in the darkness. Furniture as costly as the carpet, decorative items that were likely just as dear. His burglar's instincts twitched while his mind did an almost automatic assessment of what things would be worth, and what they might bring him should he care to steal them. But he was not here for that.

He wanted to talk to Bertie. In truth, he wanted to frighten Bertie. Underneath that need, he might also wish to kiss him. They had managed to get up to a lot of wandering, bantering, and carousing in Edinburgh, but they hadn't ever kissed, and the older he grew, the more enchanting the idea became. At eleven or twelve, he hadn't given it any thought.

When the notion came a few years later, he didn't know what to do with it, feeling somewhat like a wildcat who'd developed troublesome and inadvisable feelings for a flashy squirrel. He and Bertie were friends, and that was odd enough—he'd had to defend it, sometimes, to his rougher friends, making it clear Bertie was not a mark and could not become one. It later helped when Bertie started buying them drinks and food and the services of whoever they might fancy for a night or afternoon.

Lucas could not imagine defending a romantic arrangement, and so, he had not initiated one. From time to time, he fancied he caught a bit of desire in Bertie's eyes, but that was all he caught, and Bertie did not act upon it, either. In fact, he'd gone after Alastair readily enough, which Lucas took to mean he could have chosen Lucas if he'd wanted and merely had decided not to.

Alastair was under the impression that Lucas had gone home, but he had doubled back to Cromer after seeing off Torquil, who had adamantly wanted to go home. This country house was not far from town, and Bertie had mentioned specifically where when he'd spouted off his tales about lost Norfolk gold in The Sow.

Rage stalked Lucas' blood just as he stalked the corridor. He assumed Bertie kept his bedroom somewhere on this floor. He knew anger would not serve him as well as calm purpose, so he tried to cast it to one side. But he did resent being lied to, and he wished to know how deeply the lie ran.

There was no lost treasure, nothing to be found at the end of a long journey, and both he and Alastair had discovered that only after they had bothered to walk under the earth in a warren of tunnels that, even to Lucas with his minimal knowledge of tunneling, felt somewhat unstable. He did not, however, have minimal knowledge of breaking and entering. He moved as a ghost, peering carefully into rooms.

It came as a shock when, from behind him, Bertie's familiar, cultured voice said, "Rather an unorthodox way to make a social call, even for the likes of you."

Lucas would rather die on the spot than reveal his shaken nerves, so he composed himself with a short breath before turning to face Bertie. He eyed his old friend, applying the word because he did not know what else to call Bertie, and as it always did, his traitorous heart raced when he saw him. He endeavored to crush this sentiment as he did every other one that was not to his advantage.

Much as he had when they'd first met and he hadn't reacted to Bertie's uncanny knowledge, he tried to appear unbothered.

"Do you often take to the house in your dressing gown?" He knew he would not succeed in crushing anything, as he never had, but he also knew nobody but him would realize it.

"I am the only one here, so I don't see why not."

Of course Bertie might not see the servants as being worthy of counting. It brought another useless sentiment to Lucas' mind, namely that the young boy he had met actually *had* counted everybody, despite his upbringing, and he'd thought about those people his parents said were beneath him.

"Is it lonely?" It came out before he could think better of it. He had no fear of Bertie, but Bertie in adulthood was liable to scoff at the question.

Strangely, he did not scoff. "No."

"What is it, then?"

"Peaceful. I am the last one left, after all."

"The last one?" Lucas crossed his arms, trying for his life to look as perturbed as he told himself he felt.

"The last of my family line, as you well know."

Lucas did. After all, this old family house was what had enabled Bertie's latest little amusement, one involving lost treasure that did not exist and an acquaintance they had in common. At least in part, Lucas imagined that the house was local and that Alastair was also local had fueled something, some thirst for attention.

Lucas did not understand, and would not begin to say he could. But Bertie was fond of talking, and it was entirely possible he would learn all about why and still have very little understanding. "You *knew* there wasn't anything under that rotting old house," said Lucas, changing the subject.

"Of course."

"There weren't even any—" Lucas shook his head. "Then what, my good lad, was the point of anything?" He might never be able to fathom the rich, for all he could learn their patterns and predict their movements and steal what they held dear.

"Chaos?" Bertie's voice was mild, though a little merry.

"Could have left me well out of your chaos."

"You did not have even a little bit of fun?" Taking a step closer to him, Bertie smiled. Part of Lucas melted, while a much larger part cautioned him against melting. There might have been a bit of fun in seeing Alastair at a loss, inconvenienced, and rather without his jaunty ability to come out of anything unscathed.

"Ah, you did," said Bertie, who was watching his face in what little light the late hour afforded them, "I knew you would—did it not feel good to bring a little chaos to a man who brought you more than his fair share?"

"Even if it did, I've lost time, haven't I? Money, work."

Bertie brought a finger to Lucas' lips.

He quieted.

"I have a proposal for you, and you won't need to worry about any of that." Bertie took back his finger and Lucas willed his body to remain completely still. Despite himself, he was interested, and if it meant there might be more touching him than that of a mere finger—though he brushed the thought away like an errant bit of dust from a sleeve, the idea of being somebody's second choice irritating him—then, so much the better.

"What?" Lucas asked, making sure some derision colored the word.

"Let us go to a parlor or the drawing room. I wager you could use a drink."

"Why not just tell me what it is out here, and I can be on my way?"

He did not add that he didn't know precisely where he would go, what with Alastair assuming he had gone back on his way to Edinburgh, and he wanted to maintain that illusion. The pretty landlord would not take kindly to the suggestion of letting a room to Lucas, and although there were plenty of other places to stay within Cromer, it was not a large enough place that he could count upon remaining undiscovered. He studied Bertie's face.

Then again, Bertie had gone undetected until he wanted to be seen. But his house was not quite in the thick of things, and Lucas had to assume its location had helped Bertie remain undiscovered until he wanted to be.

"On your way where?" As ever, it felt like Bertie could read his mind when he so chose. "North? No, I need you closer—*if* you decide to take me up on this."

Curious, Lucas released a small sigh. "Go on, then, lead on to your parlor."

"Said the spider to the fly," murmured Bertie. "We shall *really* talk tomorrow. Tomorrow, we can discuss matters like gentlemen, not thieves in the dead of night. Right now, I'd like a nightcap and to smoke."

It was with a little wistfulness and much disdain that Lucas released a breath, unable to resist, yet wishing he could put up more of a protest. But some men infiltrated one's blood like a drug, and even though he had remarked to Mr. Apollyon that he'd sworn off romance, that had been done with the faintest and most treasonous of hopes that *one day* he might find it with Bertie.

## 2

———

"This place is cursed."

It was an odd sentence, but The Queen Anne was reputed to be an odd place, as humble and predictable as she might seem with her exposed beams and venerable clientele and smoke-filled taproom. There were many pubs like her, Alastair knew, or at least they appeared so at first glance. They did not have Paul Apollyon or the ferment from a family who was more than it seemed, but they functioned similarly, all little communities that served as locals for someone. He also, as though he referred to a ship, used *she* to think and speak about her. It felt correct, and in some ways, she was a little like a ship, run with discipline, a safe haven of sorts, and in need of very specific maintenance.

Alastair was well used to the number of slightly drunk people who said outlandish things in The Queen Anne's taproom by now, over a year since he had elected to remain in Cromer with Paul. He raised an eyebrow in genteel confusion and shrugged. It wasn't the most bizarre thing he had heard or experienced of late, not when he counted Lucas and Torquil's intrusion, or Bertie's penchant for twisted valentines: dead crows and ominous notes on the doors.

"She's old. Who's to say she isn't?"

Paul, who was passing behind him in time to hear this question, tutted and said under his breath, "Careful how much you tease the ones who talk about curses. They do tend to take them more seriously than not."

He kept a grin from his face as he noted his landlord's wise remark, and kept his attention on the elderly man who had spoken the ominous words. He looked as many of the local fishermen and sailors and lifeboatmen did, careworn and flushed, touched by the wind, the sea, and the sun, even when the latter was hidden behind clouds.

The man leaned over the bar and eyed Alastair intently. "I saw Old Shuck in an upstairs window."

"There's no dog here, mate."

"It wouldn't be a real one, would it? Not if it's him and not if I say your place is cursed." He held out an empty glass that smelled of beer.

Alastair supposed it would not be a real dog, not for the sake of this conversation. Old Shuck was spiritual or perhaps better said to be infernal, a great, black hellhound rumored to haunt East Anglia, stalking places like Cromer or Overstrand or Norwich, and wandering its fields and coastlines.

With his usual lack of respect for dire matters, Alastair felt he might be able to befriend such a creature, having much in common with how it initially frightened most people. Paul had pointed out in their discussions of all the folklore that, unlike Alastair, it had a prodigious number of tales and the weight of years of stories attached to it. Alastair had his looks, and if people did bother to speak to him, he was actually charming and affable.

"No, well," he said, taking the man's proffered glass and filling it up again because he did not see the harm and felt the beer might have more of a sedating effect than cutting him off would, "should we do something about it, do you think?"

He knew the public house was not cursed because he trusted those who looked after The Queen Anne. Benson, a regular customer from Paul's parents' time, was their now-resident witch-hunter. He looked like an irascible, modern version of Merlin—or what Alastair thought Merlin would look like had he lived during Victoria's reign—and saw to the preternatural threats much like poison saw to vermin. Quietly, but effectively.

That was what Paul said, and Alastair had no reason to doubt him. Surreptitiously, he glanced upwards, knowing the sigils Benson had drawn and scored into the wood were just overhead. His own sense of magic and anything preternatural was limited to sensations not unlike the breezes before storms or static charges; though he did believe in the stuff, he could not experience in the broadest sense what anyone really meant if they said they were a witch or the like.

Paul, though, he trusted with his life and more besides. Preternatural circumstances implied there was more to life than this, or that it extended past one's death. He would trust Paul in either.

"You could go upstairs and wave him off," said the man, who rubbed at his red nose and dislodged some mucus. Alastair fought off a shudder. "The likes of you should be enough to stave off Old Shuck."

Unaware if this were complimentary or derogatory, Alastair blinked and again fought against a smile. If it were the prior, he had been given better compliments, and if it were the latter, he had heard much worse, even from the man who had helped bring him into this world. The bigger he had become, the less likely his father was to insult him. But the fact remained that there had been enough barbs flung in his direction that a stranger might have to work to fling them harder—and more accurately—than his own kin had.

Benson appeared behind the old man and said, "Why, Laurence, I had no idea you were out of bed after that bout of pneumonia."

"Them doctors know nothing about a little cold," said Laurence, brushing once more at his nose.

"I'm sure you have survived worse in your time," Benson said.

Laurence passed Alastair the money for his drink; Alastair left it on the bar, hoping it would not be pressed into his palm the moment Laurence felt he had not noticed the coin. "I have. I most certainly have!"

With an arm loosely around Laurence's shoulders, the way a dog might coax an errant sheep away, Benson said, "Do tell me all about your newest grandchild," casting Alastair a look that plainly said to excuse himself.

Whatever Laurence said about his grandchild, Alastair did not know. He slipped away from behind the bar with a smirk, seeing Paul just across the room and more than able to tend to the small but lively crowd, and ventured upstairs to see what on earth Laurence had been seeing as Old Shuck.

It did not take long to hazard a guess, for in the third of their unoccupied rooms, there was a greatcoat slung over a chair left in front of one of the windows that faced the street. Someone must have left it behind, and while Alastair might have tried to abscond with it much like he had his favorite bowler hat, Paul would not condone such an act. He beamed as he ran his hand over the cloth, then tore from the room to go downstairs and then outside.

Looking up at the room's window, he reckoned it was possible, with the greatcoat and chair backlit against some weak light from the first-floor hallway, that a drunk man could easily construe the shape as being the same as a large dog on its haunches. Were he in that folkloric frame of mind and slightly delirious from abandoning his time recovering from pneumonia in favor of frequenting his local. Alastair had learned not to underestimate anyone's fondness for stories, and particularly not anyone from Norfolk, where there seemed to be at least as many stories as there were anywhere else to account for every strange noise and shadow that crept in the dark.

*Maybe Old Shuck is more underfoot this time of year.* Halloween, All Hallows, and All Saints days were indeed coming up, and even though Paul seemed to adore the macabre—fairy tales, all of which read as macabre to Alastair —he had given Halloween especially an odd sort of berth, almost as though he accorded it more respect than other old pagan days. The smile ebbed from his face when he considered why that might be, at present.

The events of the last several weeks had not been easy on Paul, and despite containing any distress with serenity, with a calm stoicism that did not allude to any of his depth of feeling, Alastair could tell he was troubled. It was writ in the way his eyes were moving more amongst the people in the taproom, and the manner in which he would no longer sit with his back to doors.

That was fair, for Bertie Calder had initiated more than his fair share of an odd little game, drawing Paul into it as surely as he had drawn Alastair, for one did not come without the other. As Alastair returned to the inside of where he had come to call home, he wished he could allay their disquiet as easily as it was to confirm Old Shuck was in fact merely a greatcoat draped on a chair, with naught but some shadows to provide its ears.

---

Lucas had a night's sleep that didn't calm him, and had waited the whole day like some man of leisure to hear what Bertie had to say. Evidently there had been some business for him to attend to, some actual business related to his newly inherited estate or some friend of his late father's, or late brother's, both of whom had been physicians. Michael had been less talented than their father, Lucas knew, but the reins needed to be passed to someone.

Michael had also been something of a sadist, pouncing on Bertie whenever it was likely to go unnoticed and trying out some weird compound or another on his little brother. According to Bertie, these incidents had only come up once Michael had gone to Cambridge, but it was bad enough in Lucas' opinion that they'd happened at all.

He'd declared several times after Bertie had finally told him the truth of things that Bertie had only to say the word and Michael could be dealt with. Of course, Bertie had never actually taken him up on it, preferring instead to spend as much time as he could out of the house whenever his brother was in residence, a practice which became easier as he grew older and more independent.

Those times felt immensely distant now as Lucas sat in a sumptuous drawing room—at least, he would call it a drawing room, though there was likely some other proper name for it; Bertie had mentioned a parlor—and waited for Bertie to explain what he wanted.

All his attempts to ignore how much Bertie still held a sway over him be damned, for his body seemed to thrum with interest now that Bertie was nearby, Lucas leaned forward in his armchair. "So, tell me more about that fucking treasure." It had felt the same in The Sow during the fateful evening when he'd seen Bertie for the first time in years.

All that had happened to draw them apart was life itself, a diverging set of circumstances that had seen Bertie go to Cambridge like his brother had, while Lucas became ever more expert at crime. They were able to meet less and less frequently, until it had been quite a while since they'd set eyes upon each other when Bertie sought him out again most recently. A short note had served as an invitation; he'd received it at the same room he'd kept for over a decade now. Bertie was inviting him to their old local.

"I really should have tried to pay you a visit the last time I was up," Bertie had said in The Sow, before they'd moved on to the topic of Trunch. "Or the time before that."

There had been a laugh in his voice, a mild titter, and Lucas realized that meant he'd been here far more often to see Alastair. It smarted. Still, he had yearned, and he'd catalogued the small ways Bertie's face had changed. Most people would not have been able to spot the minute wrinkles starting around his eyes, or rather that they were new, but Lucas could.

Almost automatically, he even continued cataloguing the differences in Bertie's appearance now. Those little wrinkles around his eyes, a very slight downward pull to his mouth, and maybe a more pronounced darkness under his blue eyes. He tried to tell himself his own attentiveness and interest meant nothing.

In truth, he wanted to know more about whatever it was Bertie had in mind for him to do, but was reluctant to give him the satisfaction of interest in anything to do with Alastair.

"What is it with you people and treasure?" Bertie exhaled smoke that smelled almost of perfume, from an elegant cigarette that Lucas had assiduously not watched him roll because Bertie's fingers could drive him to distraction. His face was obscured for a moment with the cloud, at which point Lucas allowed his own expression to look as desirous as he felt.

"Must be different for *us people* when we never had enough of anything to start with." He looked around this space, not as intensely furnished and decorated as others of its ilk, still knowing that all of its contents, if sold, might support one poor family for a pair of years. It was warm and inviting with a few candles lit, but Lucas could not quite appreciate its aesthetics when he considered their material implications.

"Well," Bertie said, having the nerve to dimple with clear amusement, "now that I know you are still here, I think we could come to a very tidy little arrangement."

"I did mean to leave, but then I decided that I wanted to

speak to you." He did not dwell on what sort of arrangement he might actually like to have with Bertie.

"Rough me up, you mean?"

Lying, lifting a shoulder in what he hoped looked like nonchalance, Lucas said, "Talk to you."

"We did have some good discussions in The Sow leading up to all this."

"Well, I wanted to better understand why you lied."

"My boy, what did I lie about?"

Reaching for the brandy in a fine crystal glass sitting on a fine little table near this fine armchair, Lucas took a sip of the stuff before he replied. "The money. The forgotten gold."

"Those stories can get so garbled, though," said Bertie, his eyes bright with the glee of teasing someone. "I did have smuggling cousins, two of whom were hanged for their troubles."

"But," Lucas said, "you *assured* us there was something." He recalled the discussion well, for it had represented the first time in a long while that he possessed some way of exacting a toll on Alastair. It was also the first talk he'd had with Bertie in ages, and God help him, he had missed Bertie. The night had passed in a pleasant haze where, somewhere in the very back of his mind, he wondered if he might be seduced at the end of it. Perhaps fantasized was a better word.

Bertie had said, rather enthusiastic about it all, precisely where to find the loot and why it had ended its journey there. There'd been a less specific tale of distant family who had met a bad end, and Lucas didn't know if they were actual people in spite of what Bertie had just said moments ago.

"You *wanted* there to be something," said Bertie.

Eying Bertie, about to make a retort, Lucas had to contend

with the words. They were almost gentle, or at least they were less smug than Bertie could be. He had indeed been desperate for there to be a manner in which he could toy with Alastair, who'd somehow bettered his entire life after that failed robbery at the Adairs' house—to Lucas' detriment.

Rather than allow himself to look too at a loss, for he trusted his ability to look unshaken with anybody but the man before him, Lucas took another sip.

"You wanted there to be something," Bertie repeated, "and I, quite frankly, took advantage of that."

"Why?" Lucas kept his eyes on the glittering crystal glass he held in his hand, idly aware he could throw it against the wall and use one of the shards to carve into Bertie's flesh if he moved fast enough, and silently admitting that was not what he wished to do. He'd felt it so often when they were younger, an urge to take this silly man to bed and make him forget, at least for an hour or two, his frigid, cruel family.

It had surprised but not utterly shocked him. He'd only been surprised because his usual way of interacting with the rich was to keep them at arm's length unless he had an aim to steal something, or wanted to laugh at what they called their difficulties because said problems could never match his own. Instead, his instinct was to show Bertie sweetness, and if sweetness was not possible, then pleasure.

Though Bertie would never admit to there being similarities between their backgrounds, they each had a similar hunger shaped by both a lack of good regard and others' cruelties. Lucas supposed part of his affinity for Bertie had started there, once he'd recognized it.

"I wanted to see what would happen."

One of the reasons they had never gone to bed was

Bertie's mercurial streak. "Did you like what you saw?" Lucas had to ask, and he could not stop himself from sounding tired when it slipped forth.

"It was certainly of interest." Again the smoke coiled from his cigarette and around him. "Are you sure you do not wish to smoke?"

*Must have been staring at his lips.* "No."

"This tobacco is exquisite."

"I'm sure," said Lucas. "Pipes are still more to my taste, though." He shook his head and finished the glass of brandy.

Bertie rose, his dressing gown gaping to expose his trim chest, and went to the decanter, walking it the short distance from the brass cart where it seemed to live, to the armchair where Lucas sat. Lucas held out his glass, used to Bertie doing such small tasks when it suited him. It had been quite some time since they had been anywhere private or domestic together, but refilling a glass or furnishing a pipe had never been beneath him.

For a fellow who had been taught connections were only for one's betterment or advancement, he was remarkably in favor of the little gestures that connected people.

"Thank you," Lucas said. He could not remember his birth parents and could not say whether they would have raised him to have any semblance of manners, as bare as they could be in his circles. All he knew was that Old Ross was somehow connected to his mother. But Old Ross had insisted on the most rudimentary of niceties, between frightening his marks to within an inch of their lives and terrorizing the local birds.

"My pleasure."

A moment passed where their eyes met, and Lucas would

have sworn he saw heat in Bertie's, but he wondered if that warmth was like Bertie's assurances that there was a sizeable amount of gold under an old farmhouse near where his family had come from, in a place called Trunch that Lucas had never once heard of and would never visit again. In short, he wondered if it was a lie.

He *wanted* the heat to be there, and so, he did not fidget, merely waited for his glass to be refilled and for Bertie to return the decanter, then take his seat again. All the while with the cigarette held elegantly between his lips.

"Why do you need me closer?" Lucas said, in an attempt to keep his mind on the circumstances at hand. "I have to say, I had no plans to stay down here after getting my hands on you." It had come out, and it had come out with a weight that did not sound right even to him, one that befit something more than intimidation. He took a long drink of the lovely brandy, which he could rarely afford and did not often drink, but still enjoyed.

"You said you wanted to talk to me." *Now* Bertie radiated smugness.

"Just like you said something was there," muttered Lucas.

"Perhaps neither of us can really trust the other, then."

"I don't know if I would go so far as to say that. I do trust you, despite all the evidence why I shouldn't. Tell me what you have in mind, and we can decide together."

"What did you think of Mr. Apollyon, when you met him?"

This was not at all what Lucas expected Bertie to say, and as far as an opening salvo went for any sort of plan Lucas might be involved in, he could not see how it followed. "Quiet sort of lad, but difficult to frighten," was all Lucas said, keeping any deeper thoughts closer for the moment, "and damned loyal to Alastair." He watched Bertie's face closely for tells of annoyance and was not disappointed when he was right to look for them.

"Yes, he is rather unexpected, is he not?" The question had an air of a man who expected a chocolate, but had bit down instead on an obscenely spicy pepper.

"You sound jealous, Bertie," said Lucas, unable to resist a jab as he swilled his brandy. The words were milder than they could have been. Lucas was reasonably sure Bertie did not entirely realize the effect he had upon him, so he had no desire to alert him to the presence of any specific feelings. Too much emotion behind a quip might complicate things, especially after his slip of the tongue moments ago.

"If he won't cede on his own," Bertie said, seemingly ignoring the mention of jealousy with the flick of an eyebrow, "I might request you to...help him along."

"What, scare him into doing what you want? Relinquishing Alastair? Telling him to leave? I do hate admitting it, but he's not very scared of me." In addition to the loyalty that flowed so clearly between Alastair and his beau, the truth remained that Mr. Apollyon seemed largely just irritated by Lucas.

"Lost your touch?"

With a scowl, Lucas glanced at the ceiling. "Something is odd about Mr. Apollyon. It's naught to do with me. He's got this strange...equanimity." Come to think of it, the entire public house had felt strange.

"Well, we could dispense with merely scaring him and consider killing him."

The sentence helped Lucas stop paying attention to the

old plaster embellishments on the ceiling and focus on Bertie. It was not the words, but instead the even tone, that drew him. He might expect it of one of his colleagues; he did not quite expect it of a relatively new-money, rich man, let alone Bertie. At least, he had never completed any violent work for someone of their ilk.

He reckoned they might suffer from the same urges as anybody and were simply too polite or removed from them to voice anything so untoward. And murder as a strategy also felt extreme in this case. After all, Bertie was not royalty or a member of government—contemplating assassination was not unheard of in matters of state. History made that clear enough. But this was merely a broken heart, and maybe not even a broken one, just bruised.

"I would consider that the last option. You might not hang for it, but I could."

To that, Bertie smiled and shook his head a little. "Only if anyone cared to catch you, and I'm not above bribery."

"Then just bribe Mr. Apollyon. Or Alastair. Why bother killing anybody?"

Then he saw the answer in Bertie's expression: satisfaction. Simply put, it would satisfy him to see his competition dead. "I've considered it. Everyone has their price. But I'm also quite taken with the idea of a less amicable option."

**3**

———————

There were few places in the world Bertie wished to visit less than Mr. Paul Apollyon's old public house. Really, he had not enjoyed watching it, either, as he found the whole idea pedestrian—what even was it, in truth? It appeared to operate as an inn or a home more than anything, though it had seemed to do brisk trade in the evenings. He tutted to himself as he stepped inside.

The main door was set away from the foyer by a little compartment meant to protect customers from inclement weather or wind, and the whole place had an air of years gone by, almost as a museum or mausoleum might. He could not understand how it could compete with any of the local hotels, but then, its usual patrons might not be the sort who could afford to go somewhere else.

He glanced around with distaste. Strange that he had not dreamt of nor seen it in a waking vision, although that just confirmed his suspicions that Mr. Apollyon was no one important. And it had to be said that, at present, he was not having quite as many visions as he normally did.

But even prior to the last few weeks, when things had been more normal and he had not yet resided in the house in Cromer, he still hadn't seen The Queen Anne in his mind's eye. He had seen Alastair visiting his home with joy on his face, and seen them lingering in bed as lovers did, and he had caught glimpses of Mr. Apollyon. But he had not been privy at all to images or experiences of the public house. As he had not been fortunate enough to have a peer or mentor with his same talents, he couldn't begin to guess why, if it came down to the location itself or some other brand of interference, or was just a coincidence of sorts.

He stepped through to the taproom, where weak, early morning sun pored through the windows, and looked around for Alastair. Only a seemingly itinerant man sat within and he looked to be asleep, dozing off in a wicker chair opposite the bar. Bertie sniffed. Such a creature should not be allowed indoors, but it paired well with the bright yellow canary that strutted above the fireplace as though it was actually the landlord.

Why it was not in a cage, and the creature was not outside, Bertie did not know.

"What are you doing here?" Alastair's quiet growl came from behind him.

He turned and smiled. "You can still sneak up on me, I see. Well, you did say to come here, did you not?"

"I was rather hoping you just wouldn't."

Because the bluntness struck him as rather funny and even charming, he chuckled, earning a frown for the noise. Alastair was in fine form today, dressed in what must have been newer clothes than any garments Bertie had once known him in, though they did look like they belonged on a fisherman rather than a more respectable person. The knit jumper was thick and untucked, and made of slightly coarse charcoal yarn. He didn't think Mr. Apollyon had knitted it, for when would a landlord find the time, but someone obviously had.

Alastair had tied his long hair back, and not for the first time, Bertie yearned to know what he would look like with it cut appropriately. Instead of commenting on his hair, he said, "Darling, what a thing to say."

"I'd prefer it if you didn't call me that."

"As you wish."

"Pardon me."

"Why?"

"You're directly where I need to walk to go put these back." Alastair gently brandished three glasses he held. "People make off with them in the evenings, and we find them in all manner of places. Unused glasses. I can't tell if they're trying to steal them, or they're so drunk they don't know that they're doing when they nab them."

"Ah," Bertie said, stepping aside just enough for Alastair to pass. "Does this life suit you? Knocking about an old public house and tidying up after drunkards?" He was curious what the reply would be.

As he went, Alastair said, "If that was all I did, I would be able to rest far more."

"Is it not frightfully boring?"

Any potential for boredom, at least from what he had observed of Alastair, might well be an issue for him, as his mind forever seemed drawn to stimulation and things of interest. It had been somewhat maddening to Bertie at the start, largely because he was used to being among the most intelligent or at least the best educated men in any given room, yet Alastair seemed to have the quickest response to anything one might say. But as they grew to know each other better, it had become one of his more endearing habits.

So very him.

Waiting until he was behind the bar to speak and leaving Bertie to follow him with his eyes, Alastair said, "No."

"You don't miss…" Bertie paused. He wanted to be careful what he evoked here. Say something about crime, and he would not be able to match or replicate that kind of excitement.

The crows were one thing; he was rather fascinated by their little lives ebbing away and flickering out under his own hands. He knew Lucas's childhood guardian, the mad butcher, had been prone to the same habit. Lucas had also murdered a few crows at Old Ross' behest, but had not ever seemed to carry the same zeal for the act. It appeared that the demimonde used them to communicate certain messages, ominous ones.

He could not quite remember everything about stalking and hurting his first one, though he was certain it had happened under the influence of something Michael had given him. His brother might even have encouraged him, for all he really knew, as his memories of that evening were scattered and not to be trusted. Rather unfortunately, his conversations with Lucas on the matter had muddled with what he thought he remembered.

Whatever had actually occurred, the crow had been left outside in the garden and Mrs. Reid assumed it had died due to some natural cause, perhaps a fight with another bird or a predator. He'd heard her telling Cook.

But the other small handful of times he had done such a thing, it had been out of agitation, then the incidents when he had meant to unnerve those inside The Queen Anne. He had known Alastair would likely think Lucas was to blame. Now he rather liked that Alastair knew he was capable of something so violent and final like killing birds.

He would not tell him about the visions of the future. Even somebody so seemingly open and accepting might well turn on him for the dubious talent. He had no way of promising that they would not and history was littered with scores of burnt witches, and people who wished to burn them. It was the modern era, one with scores of advancements that might have only been called witchcraft a generation prior, and he had more money than those poor souls could ever have dreamed of. Still, he was not keen on baring that part of himself.

"You don't miss more variety in your days?" Bertie rephrased and finished his thought.

"I have plenty." Alastair's back was turned now, his broad shoulders presenting a solid front, obscuring shelves and bottles, the great kraken tattoo on his back only creeping out from his undershirt and jumper, hinting at the art on skin beneath cloth. To Bertie, it was art, although it also had to be said that Alastair had many tattoos that could not fit the description of artistic.

The contrast between base and elevated was intoxicating, something that drew Bertie as much as any visions about Alastair ever had. In addition, Alastair was easy to covet, a far more convenient subject for his affections than alternative men: for Bertie, Alastair did not require being vulnerable and true. He did not make him feel safe or known, and therefore he required little authenticity.

Yet he did represent the sort of rakish and dashing fellow found in stories. From the time they had first met, that—and pure attraction—felt like reason enough to desire him.

"Danger, then—do you miss that?"

"No."

"Are you certain?"

"And what danger could you provide that might entice me?"

Chewing at his lip as he thought, Bertie shrugged even though Alastair could not see it. Some might say a man of his proclivities could well provide danger: the possibility of discovery, of blackmail. His parents probably had not known of his inclinations, or at least his mother hadn't. But they also had not known much about him at all, preferring to leave him as alone as possible. So long as he did not raise a fuss or draw any attention to himself.

Still, he had heard both of them pass remarks about certain men in their social milieus who were *that way inclined* and suffering some sort of consequence, generally to do with extortion or blackmail after a few hours of pleasure with the wrong person or people.

It was how he first learned the faintest ideas of where to seek companionship, should he ever want it, and in a way, he learned what not to do in order to have it without being caught. The knowledge paired well with his ability to exist without drawing any eyes to himself, learned out of necessity to avoid punishment or derision.

His brother was the son who had the attention, who

warranted it, and ironically, Michael was also the son who had died without family or issue.

And besides anything more banally dangerous, Bertie possessed the danger of something unnatural. He did not know what to name his ability to see the future, indeed, he shied away from naming it at all, but he felt it most strongly at times when he was unoccupied. An agitation, a cloying madness in the blood, some sort of energy humming beneath his skin. Bertie felt *he* was dangerous, only he neither wanted to say so nor knew how he would even begin to approach the subject.

"You would be surprised."

"I doubt it."

"Where is your landlord?" Bertie looked around as though Mr. Apollyon might appear from a shadow. "I had not thought he ever really left the premises."

"Did you want him to be here?"

With a chuckle, Bertie did not try to veil his indifference. It was fun to goad Alastair and he could tell anything less than complimentary directed at Mr. Apollyon, even in absentia, would do so. "It doesn't matter if he is, or is not."

"Well, some business required him to go out."

Bertie was, however, somewhat tired of speaking to Alastair's back. "Might we converse while meeting each other's eyes?"

On a great sigh, Alastair did turn around to face him. "I'm not sure if you want to see what's in mine."

"On the contrary, I always do."

"This is pointless, whatever you're doing," said Alastair, crossing his arms and coming closer to the edge of the back of the bar, glaring at Bertie as he did.

Thinking of the visions he had seen of Alastair in the Calders' house nearby, Bertie shook his head. "I disagree."

"Why?"

"Call it instinct."

"For my part, all you have done is waste some of my morning with useless chatter."

Beyond wishing Alastair to know he was still around and able to appear, Bertie had no other specific aim in seeing him at present. He never really did, apart from just seeing him. He also wanted to have more of a feel for the arrangement between Mr. Apollyon and Mr. Gow. It was to his deepest envy that Alastair seemed just as protective here and now over the prior, as he had that evening in the churchyard.

If he were being completely and utterly honest with himself, he might be able to see the envy was more for somebody being so very protective over him and not specifically Alastair. However, Bertie was rarely so honest with himself if it did not feel good to be so.

"Then I shall take my leave." Bertie did turn to go, but he tossed over his shoulder as politely as he could, even if it was laced with resentment, "Give your landlord my best. Perhaps I will be able to meet him one day soon."

As he walked out, he thought today might well be the day he gave Lucas what he wanted, driven by frustration and physical desire on the surface. Bertie had read his yearning since they were far younger. At first, he had not been able to acknowledge it for fear of what it might mean to his own sense of identity. Men like him, or them, were maligned or called wrong.

As it turned out, there would be no running away from the fact that he was precisely that sort of man, and over the years, he became quite accustomed to clandestine little affairs. But if he were to squint too long at his motivations to take Lucas to bed, he would grow uncomfortable with the realities that had been waiting underneath them. They were only growing harder to ignore now that he was the last of his line and had only himself to blame for the predicament.

If it could be truthful, his heart would whisper that this obsession with Alastair was a cover for the longstanding dilemma presented by disavowing himself time and time again. Repeated disavowal had stoked a need within him, one that yearned for home and acceptance, but it had also sharpened his edges to such a point that he did not know who he would be without them.

As Bertie walked back to his cab, which he had told to wait nearby, he felt that the past and present had begun to blur.

Lucas' tiny private room, which he took on his own after leaving Old Ross, was as real to Bertie as Cromer's streets. More so. They'd spent hours there, for it was clean if not snug, and even though Bertie could see a bit of embarrassment in Lucas for the setting, he did not mind. It had felt like freedom and safety, and at nineteen, he wished he could live there too, a shocking if enlightening desire.

He had never said, and Lucas had marinated in his mild and equally unspoken mortification.

They talked of anything, and sometimes might just sit in companionable quiet, insulated from the street a few floors below. The lady he let from never bothered them, either, no matter how much they laughed or raised their voices. Lucas had related more about his own childhood, which was enough to reduce a lesser man to madness but had appeared only to instill within him a deep wryness.

All the same, complete frankness was not possible; Bertie could not let it happen. How was he to bring up his uncanny premonitions, or the way he wished to touch Lucas' hair sometimes, or how, even though he tried to ignore it, he felt at peace with him in a way he could not replicate elsewhere?

Bertie was afraid to ask what sort of person he would be now if he had been honest about the intoxicating measures of security and liberty he felt in that room. He suspected he would be a happier one. Instead, he had allowed life to part them more as time flowed on. It was less of a risk to keep his sights on Alastair.

Before he could understand or name it, that chase almost felt deeper and more necessary than how peaceful he'd felt in Lucas' room. He had fallen disastrously in love with the possibility of drawing Alastair into his life, a thing he could not quite bear to do to another person or specifically Lucas. He could not entirely admit the latter to himself. Then he would have to concede how reduced and trapped he actually felt.

He was old enough now to see these patterns. Yet, his obligations chafed, and his grasp grew tighter on his visions. Depending on the moment, he was convinced his desire to keep Alastair was almost predestined, as he had in the churchyard earlier that week. Then the conviction would crumble, shaken by reality and his own heart, merely to be rebuilt again with a rebounding sensation of desperate need. This changeability was almost too much to bear, but it was the primary constant he had. He let it pull him in whatever direction it cared to, for it was familiar even if it was exhausting.

While he stepped inside the cab and settled back in his seat, the only thing he cared to interrogate much was why his visions had become so sporadic since arriving here, and if it might have to do with The Queen Anne. It felt more imperative than owning to any of the discoveries lying in wait within his mind.

***

"HE'S A DECEPTIVE ONE," said Benson from his corner, once Bertie had left.

Alastair took his first true, deep breath since he had spied Bertie lingering in the doorway to the taproom. Thank Christ Paul was out. He didn't expect an altercation to erupt between them, but he didn't fully trust himself not to resort to violence if Bertie and Paul were in the same room and Bertie flung something derisive at Paul.

"Well, yes. But we knew that."

Quite recently, because neither Paul nor Alastair could quite keep it to themselves, Benson had heard all about Bertie's machinations and would have no illusions of his gentility. For all his money, he was not especially courteous, and Alastair did not know entirely how his family had come by it, if it was new or old, or from ancestry or trade. Bertie made personal questions feel rather grotesque and invasive, though he had made some minor mention of medicine years ago. His father was a medical man, as was his brother, both of whom Bertie had been circumspect about.

The Calders, though, had style. Today, Bertie had been

dressed in a handsome suit. Alastair had no terms for the cuts of lapels or styles of collar, and he did not look at fashion plates. No doubt almost anyone would be far better able to name the type of suit Bertie wore. All Alastair knew was, there were pronounced lapels and the shades selected were light browns, probably selected under advice of a tailor. They brought out Bertie's eyes, but now the blue looked colder than it had before.

He had thought it before this moment, but something about Albert Calder had changed, only he could not say precisely what. In agreement with Lucas, he could only posit that the shift was more in the direction of bitterness and hardness. Gone was naive enthusiasm, and here were polite avarice and persistence.

"That's not what I mean. Anyone could tell you, a rich man like that one lies, whether by omission or directly."

"Then what do you mean?" Alastair was somewhat tired already of people speaking in circles, and it was not even noon.

"He makes the air shimmer."

Frowning, Alastair turned to regard Benson. "He hasn't got a drop of witchcraft in him."

"Are you so certain he doesn't?" Benson was not arguing with him; it seemed to be a genuine question.

While he could not say with absolute certainty, for who knew what anyone possessed in secret—for some, it might be desires and thoughts that they never spoke aloud, not magic —he found it so difficult to consider Bertie among the likes of Paul and Benson and even Maeve, from whose fingertips fire leaked when she was a little drunk, that the mere suggestion made him balk. Never had there been any evidence of such a talent.

Although Bertie did repress and ignore so much, Alastair could not think witchery was among the things he kept a distance from, because such a fanciful topic had never really come up at all. It felt more like Bertie had never so much as thought about the subject of witchcraft, not that he had ideas on the topic and was trying not to acknowledge them. Still, there was that odd little habit of sleep-talking. He considered this briefly, knowing that for Paul, that was sometimes evidence of a premonition.

He humored Benson a little as Alma padded across the room and hopped onto his table, a black shadow of fur with yellow eyes ambling on the wood. "What sort?"

"That, I can't say." Benson stroked the cat with gentle fingers and she started up a purr. He and Alma got on so well, Alastair had begun calling her his familiar. "The impression was faint. Like hearing a quiet conversation through a thick wall."

"Could it not be The Queen Anne? Her...everything we are?"

Ever since the slightly drunk Laurence had insisted that Old Shuck was upstairs in a window, they had been toying with calling it The Shuck instead. But Paul ruefully noted that it might well keep some suspicious types away, and so they had only given her the pet name in private. Really, it felt apt and dry humored, less a curse than a sly little nod to the rather unusual landlord and his tolerance for the equally weird. On the other hand, Benson thought it a splendid idea, but he also was not the best indication of what would do well for business.

"Ambient magic?" Benson resettled his stained, old hat, which might have suited a farmer in the last century. Alastair had no notion of where he had found it. Though it was some kind of cloth, probably a waxed cotton of a rust shade, it had the shape of many straw sun hats. Very strange thing to favor indoors, and a very odd thing to wear in autumn.

"Yes, or yours." As he said it, he realized that for Benson's own magic to be showing in the air, someone else must be provoking the reaction. All of Benson's witchery, or all that he had been told about here, was intended to protect. It might be reacting to Bertie. "Perhaps not yours."

He sighed and untied, then clumsily retied his hair to give himself something to do with his hands. It did not follow that Bertie was preternatural, so the thought did not disturb him any more than Bertie himself did. Which, in truth, was rather more than he would have thought. The circumstances were disturbing, as they had begun to be when the first crow was nailed to the door and Lucas came unannounced to the taproom, claiming Alastair owed him.

Alastair's life, now so lovingly arranged, was being upended by naught but a spoiled rich boy who was upset Alastair had not registered the presence of finer feelings when they went to bed. In his own defense, it was not as though he could not possess them himself. It was more that he had not had the space to explore or nurture them. All of his feelings seemed larger and louder than others' emotions. As such, he generally tried to keep some distance from them, despite loving a good romance or gothic novel as much as the next person.

Then Paul had slipped so seamlessly into his senses that all he knew these days were finer feelings. He did not have the time or inclination to nurse Bertie's, and particularly not after he had heedlessly meddled in a life that had nothing to do with him at all.

*But that's the trouble, isn't it?* It was nothing to do with him, which offended him.

Alastair refocused on Benson, who lounged in his chair with slightly reddened eyes and a keen gaze. "He's just angry I didn't fall in love with him, the way he did me. Maybe his rage is making the air eddy."

For his part, Benson merely shrugged. "There are those whose feelings do that. It's magic of a kind, though nothing with much power if it's not directed. They might cause something to fall off a shelf with their minds, or some silly thing like that."

"Of course there are," said Alastair. "And it would be just my luck that I happened to mortally offend one of them." For he would not want even a glass to fall from a shelf if Paul were anywhere nearby Bertie's emotions.

**4**

___

Paul Apollyon was not having the best of evenings upon hearing Mr. Albert Calder had paid The Queen Anne a visit. "I should see if Benson can somehow deter him from the premises." He did not know if such a thing was possible via witchcraft, but he would be willing to go to great lengths to keep the man out of his establishment. Looking around his empty taproom, he forced himself to consider if his ire was an overreaction.

If he disregarded all that had happened, especially since Lucas entered The Queen Anne with an unceremonious determination, it was as peaceful as it ever had been. The end of a working night, and the three lodgers had taken to their rooms. Two other customers had required rooms as well, and they were nowhere to be seen, likely having gone to bed, too.

Paul could not disregard everything for more than a moment. Alastair did not seem to think *Bertie* was as much of a threat as he himself did. But Alastair had been his lover and was still the focus of all his affection. If it could be called such. Were he not the focus of something, they would not be in this precise situation, with Paul feeling distinctly unsafe in his home and on the streets where he had grown up. Bertie was not in the middle of Cromer, his home being somewhere outside the edges, but it was close enough for him to have walked here.

If he had not walked and had taken a cab, it was still too close. He had at least two other homes, Paul was sure, and why he could not simply live in one of those was a mystery. They knew why, or why on a superficial level. He was on some mad quest to...*Win Alastair over?* Paul was not sure what, precisely, Bertie attempted to do.

That Alastair would not be swayed was clear, or so they both thought, and Alastair could not explain with much confidence what it was Bertie wished to prove. Paul had an underlying assumption that Bertie was not entirely sure himself; though ghoulish and calculated to a point, the behavior also felt erratic. As a great observer of people, Paul had seen and heard a great many things about what they did when unresolved feelings lingered under the surface.

They could fester, and it seemed they often did. He tried not to let his own stagnate. Not for the first time in the last few weeks, Paul thought with revulsion of the life Bertie could offer Alastair, should Alastair entertain Bertie's infatuation seriously.

Paul did not see the wealth, or the ease. *Whatever else Bertie is, he is wealthy.*

He saw a lie, the sort of arrangement where Alastair was little better than a favorite pipe one brought out at night—but pipes were not generally smoked amongst polite company. For that, if the metaphor were to make any sense at all, a man like Bertie would want a wife. *Well, not want.*

"If he could, I would still have to talk to him somewhere else."

"Have to?" Paul looked up from the grain on the old wooden table. Like many of the bits of furniture the Apollyons had collected over the years, this was worn and well taken care of, and nobody now living could say precisely what sort of wood it was, it being so stained by years of tobacco smoke and continuous use. A connoisseur could, he was sure, but he was no expert in antiques.

Alastair resettled his weight in the chair opposite Paul's. "No. I don't have to do anything. But he is persistent, and until he decides to go away or I force him to—"

"Any idea when that will be?"

"I don't know."

This was mystifying to Paul, who felt a man interested in nailing dead crows to public house's doors—his public house's doors—should not be tolerated beyond the barest interactions, if at all. The main thing that might make some sense was lingering loyalty, which Paul was not convinced Alastair possessed in this case. He had seemed more bewildered than anybody when Lucas relayed how Bertie felt about him.

That walk from Trunch through Overstrand and back to Cromer felt as though it had happened years ago, though it had only been a few days. Despite knowing loyalty was not the issue, Paul found himself asking, "Do you still have feelings for him?" Alastair appeared so offended by the suggestion that Paul felt compelled to recant slightly. "I don't mean to say they are like what you have for me."

"I feel pity for him."

As a log crackled softly in the hearth at the far end of the taproom from where they sat, Paul waited for Alastair to elaborate. He could not muster such a kind emotion for Bertie, although he usually found it easy to summon empathy for most people. Whether it was learned through his time helping his parents with all sorts of customers in a public house, or he was an empathetic person naturally, he could not decide. Perhaps they were one and the same.

Bertie roused a deep, hot disdain, and that was largely all.

"I feel like he only got to form halfway," said Alastair, "like, despite all of his privilege and wealth, he was stunted by society's expectations and his family's lack of warm regard for him."

This surprised Paul, who had not expected such a philosophical reason. "Lucas mentioned his brother had finally died. I imagine most of the warm regard was for the elder son, with little for the younger."

It felt antiquated in the modern day to utter the words *heir and spare*, but he supposed for some families the sentiment still held true and for the unlucky spares, there would be no excess love or affection. And if Bertie's proclivities were for other heirs and spares rather than daughters, that would add another layer to his feeling less-than, inadequate, superfluous.

Or so Paul imagined. He was so far removed from that way of being, he may as well be musing about the moon, and he did not want to humanize Bertie much.

"From what Bertie and Lucas both alluded to, yes."

"On that, are you quite certain Lucas and Bertie never, well, took each other to bed, or..." Paul cleared his throat. He could be lewd. But it still felt too strange to be explicit in a room where he was taught to comport himself with more dignity than the customers often had.

With an air of amusement, Alastair shrugged. "He did seem a little envious of me, did he not, as we walked, and he described what had happened to get him dragged into it all."

"I think he either wanted to have him as a lover, or he did, at some point."

"Yes."

Indeed, Paul had thought so, but he would never have felt comfortable enough to ask Lucas or even make a quip about it. "I did hear a little of what could have been envy. He seemed rather territorial."

On a grin, Alastair said, "We may never know, and I pray never to see Lucas again, so may we *truly* never know."

"Do you pray?" Prayer seemed like too desperate of an act for Alastair.

"I took up the practice after I met you. If there is a god, he gave me something to be properly thankful for, for once."

From any other man, Paul might have thought it was a sweet lure, just meaningless words meant to entice him. But from Alastair, it was sincere, and he could not help but lean over the table and reward him with a kiss for the sincerity.

---

Lucas quite thought the world had gone mad.

He could not say precisely how because it was all an enchanting blur for him, but he was in Bertie's bed. Delicious as it was, he was also slightly confused and angry, unclear on how the discussion had even led to being in bed like this. Secondarily, *now* was the moment Bertie had decided to move on him, and the timing was a source of irritation. It was all consensual, so he was not concerned about whether either of them wished for this.

He did want to press more at Bertie's motives, but feared if he questioned this too much, it might be cheapened in some way. Heaven help him, but he cared and did not want what had just happened to be tarnished by trying to make sense of it. He knew he was not Alastair, for a start, and that was bad enough when Bertie's preference was already so clear.

Bitterness rose in his chest with an almost physical ache when he thought about that too long. It was more an obsession than a preference, and Lucas was curious to know why it had taken root so strongly.

But that curiosity was muted by his longstanding tendre for Bertie, even if he would not speak of it. Indeed, all the world around him seemed to deride any softer feelings—even if they were in a girl's direction, which for him, they could be. He could be attracted to anybody. He brushed aside memories of Old Ross saying it was better to succumb to drink than a woman, for the woman could leave and the drink would always be there. A man might present the same situation.

Inhaling, he rolled to his side and looked at Bertie, whose eyes were closed and head was on the opposite pillow. "What were we talking about before we got here?"

Bertie had not fallen asleep. He could tell by the rise and fall of his chest in the lamplight. But the answer was still slow. "Bickering, not talking."

"Normal for us." Now there was even more *us* than there had been.

"You wondered why I could not just leave your compatriot alone."

"Alastair isn't my compatriot. Hasn't been for years."

"He was."

"Not since he left Edinburgh, at least." Before then, in truth, when Lucas began to suspect him of ruining the robbery at the Adairs' home in New Town. Now, Lucas understood that it had not been intentional so much as the result of a stray good deed. Envy trickled through there, too, for it seemed no matter which road he took or wanted to take, someone else had beaten him to it and he would be forever relegated to whatever might be left.

Bertie opened his eyes, revealing that cursed bright blue, and smiled. "No, I expect you were done with him when you walked into that old eccentric's drawing room and found it empty."

Even Bertie made reference to the Adairs' love of old, valuable things and the housebreak gone wrong. Well, Lucas had spoken to him about it at the time, only in passing, but enough to insinuate Bertie's special favorite had likely been the man who ruined it. At the time, no one had known for certain, but it had been suspicious that Alastair, who was never moneyed enough to turn down jobs, was suddenly able to be more choosy about what he did.

"Fine," said Lucas, raising his eyebrows, "but why did you seduce your way out of bickering? We've squabbled many a time, and this is the first time I've made a mess in your bed about it."

"Why not?"

Lucas did not want to be a *why not*. He was not well versed in love, and in fact, he did not know if he could name it. But it felt like he was in love with Bertie Calder despite all his attempts not to be, or all his tries at ignoring how his blood warmed when Bertie was near. Bertie had not been the only person he ever found attractive. But Bertie was the only person who had roused this vexing and unbidden response.

Lucas had half a mind to slip out tomorrow and warn Paul Apollyon, not because he thought Alastair would be tempted away. The new sort of bitterness he could sense from Bertie seemed like it would not tolerate a competitor. Lucas sensed it would not matter if Alastair stated his own desires once or a hundred times; Bertie would not listen. He could not say why, though if he spent enough time with Bertie, perhaps he could learn what had caused the change. But he wagered he might be able to stand as an alternative to Alastair whenever Bertie was through trying to have him.

He never had possessed high standards for himself when it came to intimate relations, and he was not about to begin now that Bertie appeared to want him for whatever the reason. The highest standard involved diseases, and Bertie did not have any. In that, Lucas trusted him.

Loyalty and tenderness did not seem to be for him, though he did hold out hope some could be found, so he would lie. "That's the spirit," Lucas said.

"And to answer your question from an hour ago, I don't want to leave Alastair alone."

"Of course you don't."

Bertie stroked a hand along his arm. "Are you envious?"

That, he would not lie about. He felt a great many things for Alastair and not all of them were bad. But most of them were, and there were too many there to pretend it was not complicated. "Yes."

"I think that works in my favor."

"Why?" Lucas asked, as Bertie's fingertips trailed along his skin, warmer than whisky down his throat on a cold night.

"If you were not, I think you would tire of my objectives."

"Your games, you mean."

"He may think he wants a life in that awful little public house now, but he won't always."

Sighing, Lucas said, "You said you wanted me to step in. Do you still want that? I do assume so."

"I want functional muscle."

Not without a frame of reference for what that meant, Lucas gazed at him. "You really do want me to hurt somebody when—not if—he's stubborn."

Bertie nodded once, his blond hair mussed against the pillow and bright as his eyes.

"He's in love with that Apollyon, you realize."

"Is he?"

"I haven't the faintest idea of what being in love is like, but I do reckon so." Obscuring the truth came easily, even when speaking to the person whom it concerned.

It was in their eyes, their voices, the way they had constantly deferred to each other in an ebb and flow like the tides nearby Cromer. He might not say it looked easy, and with Alastair's past, it would never be easy for Mr. Apollyon, but it looked enticing. Where he would have expected Bertie to turn a bit ferocious with jealousy, there was only a faint and almost benign amusement in his expression, as though he knew something was going to happen that nobody else could ever see until it did.

"He is a companionable man, but I think he confuses good regard for love."

This felt odd to Lucas, because as far as he had known, Bertie had only ever observed them from covert places near the public house. He had never met the landlord, though he had now visited the premises. "As your friend and someone who clearly doesn't mind being your second choice"—even though he did mind it—"I hope you're correct. For the sake of your dreams." It was hard not to sound acrimonious, but he thought he kept most of it out of his tone.

"I don't want you to do anything much to Alastair," said Bertie. "But if necessary, I may look the other way if something needs to happen to his *beau du jour*." He said it with the same face as someone remarking on their second favorite hat, and Lucas had to chuckle with some disbelief.

"Well, at least I know where your sudden attentions have come from."

Bertie said, "I have no wish to cause you offense or take advantage of you. I would never promise undying loyalty, but I am happy to keep this sort of arrangement—"

Too unnerved by how amenable he was to this, Lucas finished the thought. "Until you get what you want."

"Quite so. There, you see? No lies, no illusions."

Lucas doubted that was true, and if he allowed his gut any range within this discussion, it said to him that Bertie was mired in lies and illusions.

Whatever he had been, it was now veiled and driven by little more than a singular interest in a man who did not want him at all. Unluckily for Bertie, Lucas had come of age in a web of little but cruel deceptions. He could bide his time and decide to change course if something did not suit him.

He was also willing to wait and see if the Bertie of old came to the fore, because Lucas could still sense him lingering there under the surface. He knew when men were concealing things; interrogation had been one of his specialties because he was soft spoken and, he was told, rather intimidating in his appearance despite being rather slight.

Instinct told him that Bertie was withholding something—information, motivation, the key to this militant and senseless gameplaying. If Lucas wanted him, he needed to get to the root of what was withheld. *What are you hiding, Bertie?*

## 5

"If he is going to come back, and I think he will, I reckon you might be happier removing yourself for a little bit." Alastair was not supposed to say it, but he did, and evidently there was nothing Paul wanted to hear less because his lovely face contorted into a frown.

Fidgeting from foot to foot in a small manner, Alastair found he could not look away from him, but he had to move or go a little mad in an attempt at stillness. Fortunately, the kitchen was well traversed during the day, and it was past noon. Molly would come and interrupt their discussion; he counted upon it.

"Seeing Muriel and Abigail holds no appeal, which I have already said before now, and neither does going to see Edward."

"I'm not sure what is actually wrong with Bertie, as *I've* said," said Alastair, drawing on patience he could enact best for Paul, "but he isn't easily dissuaded."

"Have you tried rumpling one of the rugs so that he trips?"

It merited a smile, one Alastair felt bloom over his lips like a shy spring daffodil. "I could do more than that, but it might mean more obfuscating than we want to do." This discussion had started innocently enough, from a letter that had arrived earlier that morning, one in which the elder Apollyon sibling, Edward, had asked after an old trunk of his effects.

Letters rarely led to good things for Alastair.

The trunk was still here, of course, as Alastair imagined very little of the family's effects ever left the building, and it was positioned under one of the taproom windows looking out at the street. Presently, it was layered with quilted pillows made by a dear old woman who had bartered them for a bit of blue ruin. Customers sat on it, oftentimes.

"Where is your head, in all of this?" Paul asked.

This was a valid question, and Alastair did not know quite how to answer it. October had not been kind to them, or it had not been as predictable as the other months he had spent here, and his head was full of visions of ghosts—or just the ghost of his wife—and old colleagues come to call, and past decisions bleeding from his former life and into this one.

Never mind all the recollections of mediocre sexual acts with Bertie, none of which were forced, but most of which were done from Alastair's perspective as by rote. Like making a bed.

He did not know and might not ever understand where Bertie's fervor came from, or how he had changed from a somewhat vapid lad to the hardened man he was now. It was not the same hardness one could find in men on the street; this felt sharper than that, something more akin to the thinness of a knife's edge than an unrelenting bedrock under years of poverty and insecurity.

"I hardly know, angel." He sighed. It was difficult to ebb and flow through life with another, and to be asked such a question and admit he did not know the answer aloud. But he would not trade his time with Paul for anything. "That's part of the trouble."

"Trust yourself more, then," said Paul, leaning across the wide table used to prepare meals, eyeing Alastair. "Your instincts are always good, or they have been as long as I have known you."

In truth, whether they were was also in question. "I settled down here; I brought an apparent madman to your door."

"You didn't know he was mad."

"I told him to come to The Queen Anne. When we talked outside the church." Alastair rubbed at his scalp, toying reflexively with hair that was wild today, even by his standards. It looked like the canary had been making a home on his head, though it was happily upstairs in the landlord's flat and was not in the habit of playing in anybody's hair, despite now being tamer and more congenial with humans than any other pet bird they knew of. It even had reached a truce with Alma, who still had not eaten it or made it into a toy.

"I think you panicked."

"It's not my public house—it's yours," said Alastair, "and you deserve to feel safe here."

"I do. Mostly," was the soft reply, paired with a gentle touch of Paul's hands when he reached across the space over the table to still Alastair's own, "I do feel safe here, when it comes right down to it. Do I still wish he could be barred?

Yes. I suppose I could do that. Tell the authorities and make sure they know." Paul stroked at his wrists. "I don't know what it would really accomplish, as he seems to think himself above rules and decency."

"At least Benson's bewitchments seem to be doing something protective."

"I'd feel even better if something in the material world could do the same."

Left unspoken was the influence of class and standing: Paul was not poor or unknown in the community, but Bertie was both rich and from a family with relatively new money from the turn of the last century.

Knowing or guessing Paul was also thinking of the crows, Alastair huffed and attempted to relax under his touch. "Like a twisted Jack Valentine, he brings things to the door."

Smiling small but genuine, Paul shook his head. "I think you're rather taken by those stories. I shall have to watch myself come February, or you'll find a way to leave me all sorts of presents on the night of the thirteenth. Better you than Bertie, though. You would choose something I enjoyed."

As ever, Paul was correct and he was thinking about stories; last night, Alastair, struck by a bout of insomnia, had risen to sit in the parlor in the landlord's flat rather than disturb Paul's sleep.

Instead of remaining abed, Paul came out to join him and told him stories, stroking his hair when Alastair put his head in his lap, and insisting he shut his eyes.

The tales of choice were about Jack Valentine, a figure who left gifts the night before Valentine's Day, and Alastair could not decide if the idea was ominous or whimsical. It was a bit of both, to be fair, and far more likely that it was sweethearts carrying on the tradition rather than some mystical or preternatural being. Then again, seeing as he was living with a seer, perhaps that was an incorrect assumption. Facts were only ever as good as their realities, so who was to say a gentleman with the ability to be stealthy and quick enough on his feet to visit the homes of such an impressive number of people in one night did not exist at all.

In Bertie's case, though, he supposed he should be thankful there had been no further morbid valentines—no more notes or dead birds—or the new appearance of any more proper gifts. He would not be swayed by valuables or trinkets, and as he had said to the man in question, he did not need money.

Paul did not pay him because he wouldn't let it occur, as he felt he wasn't an employee, but he had enough of his own resources to be comfortable for some time yet. Even accounting for a son whose upkeep he would continue to meet, whether out of kindness or latent guilt. He still was unsure if it was ethics or shame that kept him most invested in sending money north to James.

With a soft rustle of cotton skirts, Molly entered the room with her usual furtive glance at Alastair and he stepped aside as Paul relinquished his hands. Everyone in The Queen Anne knew about them, or everyone who was employed or lived there did, and none took issue with their affections. But they presently impeded her access to the table.

She said, mostly to Paul and almost as much to Alastair, "It has gone around that you want to rename the place." Her umber eyes seemed to hold more laughter than her expression did as she settled some onions next to a parsnip. She bore a small box of various vegetables, which she set gently on the tabletop once she could. "And Maeve wonders if you will really call it The Shuck."

"Renaming pubs happens often enough," said Paul, "and it's not as though it is bad luck, like renaming a ship."

"Naming it after Black Shuck might be."

If Molly herself was frightened of this, Alastair could not tell. She was shy, he knew, and she was gradually growing used to him, but it didn't seem to signify anything bad to her. If he had his guess by her calm expression and nearly friendly tone, she was perhaps a little tickled by the idea of calling her place of work after a folkloric beast.

In an endearing manner, Paul tilted his head slightly, much like their inherited canary did when it paused between chirps, and appeared to give her words a little thought. "My parents might have stopped me, if only to appease the elderly or superstitious. I suppose some of the lifeboatmen and fishermen would hate it, now that I think about it."

Molly had come after Paul's parents' time, but she was local, knew the ways of some of her fellows, and nodded. "My father talks about Shipden, and Old Shuck...to him, they're only stories that get told this time of year. But my grandfather, that's my mother's father, he was a lifeboatman and took all of it to heart."

Alastair thought he must be gaining some of Molly's trust if she was divulging so much. He listened until she quieted, having heard her speak more to the cook and Miss Garland, whose mother had been a friend of her mother, than anybody else. She offered Paul a little shrug, as though to say there was no accounting for superstition, and continued to withdraw the contents of her box.

She said, "Although, in some of the things I've heard, Old

Shuck is almost friendly... more like a real dog. Who is to say?"

With a sigh, aware his moment to press Paul into a visit elsewhere had come to an end, Alastair said to him, "We'll revisit the discussion later."

"No," Paul said, serenity flowing from him.

Biting his lower lip to stop a smile, Alastair shook his head, knowing the only person who might be as stubborn as he was stood before him in a well-loved kitchen, discussing renaming a pub while his employee offered mild opinions on local superstitions and set out onions in an orderly fashion.

HE WAS GROWING tired of bad dreams, natural or otherwise. Paul had the sense that somewhere outside of this scene, he was still in bed asleep.

Lucas stood before him on an expanse of grass that didn't seem rural or overgrown, so much as tended to as part of a house or villa. Paul frowned, having more than one or two questions to ask him, and opened his mouth, but no sound came forth. Cloth over his lips, verging just into his dry mouth. He tried to move his arms, which he had thought were at his sides. Upon further reflection, they were bound behind his back.

Intrigued only by the thought of this being a premonition, because it had the same fluid lucidity as they generally did, he resigned himself to studying Lucas's face. He hoped the man was well away by now, perhaps up to something nefarious in Edinburgh, but there were no promises he wasn't still skulking around nearby.

While his mouth was gagged, his nose was uncovered and revealed nothing to him save the usual damp earth and salt from the sea, which must be somewhat nearby; this field or lawn did not seem close to the beach for he could not hear the waves, but it smelled adjacent.

Lucas looked just as he had when Paul last encountered him, which was to say unremarkable and redheaded and blessed with the same long scar near the corner his mouth, slanted up his cheek. His clothes were unchanged, too, presentable in a tradesman's way, and as seemed to be his habit at times, he did not have on a hat.

What he clutched in his left hand caught Paul's attention more than his manner of dress: a limp crow. He held it up unceremoniously and said, "You have to stop him, you see?"

The trouble was, Paul did see, and he did not especially want to see more than this. Through nothing but the deepest desire to wake, he jarred himself away from the scene and was relieved to open his eyes to nothing but his bedroom in the dark, a sight that was familiar and reassuring. With Alastair dead to the world at his side, he felt a little better, but he ran a hand across his mouth and contemplated what sort of dream that had been.

If it was a harbinger, perhaps he ought to be on the lookout for their friend from the north and any spare fabric that could be used to wind around someone's head and mouth. Rope, too. It did call into question the veracity of the vision he'd had only days ago, in which he'd been plunged through cold, dark water while bound.

Or perhaps it did not call anything into question.

He hadn't been gagged in that one, and if it were to come to pass, he might be gagged right up until the moment he was not. His ability to see forward in time, if that was the correct assessment of what he could do, was not always orderly or easy to understand. At times, he saw multiple versions of the future and at others, he witnessed things more like preternatural allegories: scenes that only made sense after some space was between him and what had passed. Then he could trace and tie metaphors or allusions to more concrete events.

His mother slicing her open palm in the kitchen had been reflected in one mercifully short, childhood vision that had been nothing but a lurid red rose whose thorns dripped with a little blood.

A ten-year-old Paul had not understood what it might have conveyed until, a month later, she'd caught herself with a breadknife, and on the windowsill behind her, there had stood the same beautiful rose in the exact same vase as was in the vision.

Or he'd just looked for meaning in nothing.

Hands trembling, he sat up slowly and got out of bed. He had to check the doors for crows, and he did not want to bother Alastair with what might well be only a nightmare. He hadn't thought Lucas would want to linger, and he knew they were Bertie's handiwork. But if the last fortnight or so had taught him anything, it was that appearances and assumptions were deceptive while such dark valentines seemed to find their way to his pub.

The floorboards barely creaked under his weight; he knew where to step as innately as he knew breathing, which was to say it came automatically. Sighing, he took a banyan from the hook on the door and eased it onto his naked body. Highly unlikely that anybody would be wandering the corridors at this hour, but in the event they were, he had to maintain some illusion of decency. He also stepped into his slippers, knowing the floor would be cold on bare feet.

Silence permeated the landing outside his flat, but quiet in The Queen Anne was never totally still. The distant sound of waves was always there, varying in intensity depending on how close to any windows one was, as were human noises of breathing and coughing. Clocks joined the chorus, too, though they were not something his ears often registered.

By the time he reached the ground floor, he was almost willing to concede that he might be succumbing to paranoia. His home always had that calming effect on him; he supposed he was lucky to have such a place in his life when so many did not. Alastair, was part of that serenity now, though he might try to deny it if Paul ever said it.

With relief, he discovered there was no corvid affixed to the back door that opened into the kitchen. If any neighbors were awake at this ungodly hour, he wondered if they might see the door opening and closing, even if they could not see him against a backdrop of the dark indoors. He chuckled, knowing that would not help the strange rumors that sometimes swirled around his family.

Moving through the kitchen, then the hallway, then finally the taproom, he prepared himself to open the front door. The dream had not been long, or he did not recall all of it, but it had a disarmingly heavy quality.

In truth, he was confused, for it lacked neither the clarity of a premonition nor the fluidity of an organic dream. A premonition might lack input from certain senses, but it always felt true to him in a way he struggled to put to others. A dream, on the other hand, might be permeated with detail and yet lack that ring of truth. He also, like anyone, probably didn't remember all his dreams. He did recall the premonitions.

Exhaling before he did, he unlocked and opened the door. No crow. Still, Lucas' soft question lingered in his ears, and he was not certain he wished to admit or confirm who *he* was.

THE ENTIRE TIME he had spent in Cromer, Bertie's dreams had been numerous and voluminous, but they had not rung like visions. They felt real, not at all like the lurid hum of time and fate that underpinned premonitions. At first, he'd ascribed it to getting better sleep near the sea because he always had slept better near the ocean. Then he'd had to remind himself of all the times he had slept in this house and had either no dreams—if he were with Michael and his parents, Michael's presence was never conducive to sound rest—or the normal number. Some of which might be of the future, or versions of the future. But all the same, most of these present dreams fit a pattern of what others might describe as normal.

As he breathed quietly on his back in bed and gazed up at the ceiling, he thought it strange that this time, his mind seemed to be more active and causing him to dream. That had to be the cause. He really was more activated, more thoughtful, even if some might say more scheming, than he had ever been as a child or younger man.

He blinked, playing through what he had seen in his mind's eye again.

Mr. Apollyon on the nearby beach, soaked to the skin in

all his clothes, strewn with what might have been sea grass or weeds. Lit with the hues of a sunset and standing on that empty beach, he merely looked at Bertie and said a sentence in the same accent Bertie always tried to shed, the one Michael began to mock as soon as he was off to Cambridge and did his best to lessen, too.

All Mr. Apollyon said was, "You have to stop."

Then, within the space of a blink, Mr. Apollyon became Michael as he'd been on his deathbed, pale and drawn with cracked lips, only he stood on that same beach instead of remaining recumbent under covers. Bertie had woken up after that blink had changed the slight landlord to his diminished elder brother. He did not know what Mr. Apollyon meant and he was reasonably confident the dream was no vision; how could it be with one of the parties being already dead by his hand?

If not by his hand physically, then indeed his will, for he had put more than enough laudanum in Michael's tea to ease the pain of two ailing men.

It had not been something he had agonized over; it had, in point of fact, been remarkably easy to tip his hand longer than was necessary and bring his brother the tea in question.

There was no one but him to care for Michael and there was no one in the London house but them. Michael had not rushed to marry because he enjoyed the city's less respectable pursuits, those incompatible with a family life, though they were less incriminating than Bertie's pursuits. Gambling, drinking, general carousing.

As such, there was no wife or child present, and there was also no trustworthy butler or anybody underfoot in the house during the evening to provide Michael with any medicated tea. He had let go of the servants their parents had favored, bothering only to keep a few who came in the morning and left at night.

He was horrendous at managing both people and resources. The shortcoming, in addition to Michael's love for high-stakes wagers and his tendency to be hedonistic, had meant becoming a properly respected medical man with a queue of wealthy patients was beyond him. He'd scraped by in his studies without entirely disgracing himself or fully disappointing his mentors.

But his clients were neither especially moneyed, nor the sort of people who might bring him better clientele. He most often treated people for problems they were embarrassed to discuss with their family physicians, including venereal diseases. The lack of success was what Michael deserved.

Bertie's money had been set aside for his own use, and he lived very comfortably, but he did not know what to expect after Michael's death. He had possessed some notion that access to every bit of family money was contingent upon certain factors such as marriage. Though he had lied and told Alastair he had all of it, he had most of it. Still, his *most* was many people's idea of a fortune. Bertie suspected that Michael could have manipulated his way into securing everything, which meant it might have been squandered.

It was a surprise when Bertie found that everything from bank accounts to property was present and correct. All had been as it should be. Michael had been belligerent with his household servants, but nobody else, including the Calders' various bankers, solicitors, and bookkeepers.

He exhaled deeply. He had not murdered his brother for money.

In actuality, he could not quite say why he had. He only knew the death did not scream murder, what with Michael having suffered from a feverish flu, then pneumonia. He was safe from suspicion. Nobody but him had been in that house, and no authorities would have any reason to think ill of him.

Shuddering, he tried not to acknowledge how alike they had looked and instead gazed around the familiar bedroom, trying to ground himself in lavish furnishings and familiar, musty scents. When it became clear some moments later that he would not be able to go back to sleep, he rose and put a smoking jacket on over his nightshirt. A chill had taken hold, not intolerably, but noticeably. His feet led him, through the dark, to Lucas's door. He did not need any light to navigate the house, which he knew better than his own mind at present.

The hurt on Lucas's face earlier had been plain enough to him, even if Lucas had worked to obscure it, and he knew his friend wanted more than pleasure with him. Whether Lucas could admit it was another thing, and Bertie imagined it would go against a lifetime of denial.

Their upbringings and positions in life *were* different; there was no way around it. And Old Ross, who had served as Lucas's guardian until Lucas could fend for himself, bore brutality more deeply than anybody of their acquaintance. Lucas never discussed it with any depth, and the omissions weighed more heavily than any confidences he might have shared.

He remembered seeing Lucas' cheek heavily bandaged for the first time, one morning when they had agreed to meet while Bertie was at his leisure. This was before he took a place at Cambridge, and just after Lucas had left Old Ross' home. Otherwise, had they still been living together, Bertie might have assumed Old Ross had been the cause of it.

That was the type of man he was.

But off Bertie's unspoken question, the only reason Lucas had given was a brusque, "Broke up a fight." He must have looked horrified; despite being more accustomed to hearing about the perils of Lucas' life by then, seeing something so stark felt worse.

Despite any of their dissimilarities, like Lucas, Bertie knew intimately the tension present in never discussing parts of oneself. He yearned to be seen, and yet could not bring himself to own what he was. What he could do. How visions paraded around him.

He had not even told Lucas what he had done to Michael, and Lucas might understand better than anyone else he knew. His hand went to the doorknob and rested there, the brass cold and grounding under his palm. After long moments, he did not turn it, but still he kept his hand there.

If he opened the door, what then? If he sought true solace with someone besides Alastair, it would undermine everything. He would not go so far as to think it would change the course of his visions, or maybe it was more accurate to admit he did not want the visions to change, those scenes of Alastair in this house and with him.

Lucas had to mean nothing, or Alastair would mean nothing. Yet there were moments in his and Lucas's shared history strung like pearls, soft and shining ones that might, if he let them, dissuade him from the path he was on. They had often shared an awareness that felt innate. It was irksome at times, as well. Still, always something of a touchstone, even if Bertie was wary of acknowledging it existed.

He was far more likely to play with Lucas, as he had when supplying so many details about Trunch, than he was to be frank with him. But when Lucas had been stalking through his house and Bertie came upon him, recognizing him by tread and smell before sight confirmed who it was, he'd been unexpectedly and immeasurably happy for a moment before he forced the happiness back down.

Lucas could not be what he truly wanted, not after all this time. He edged away from the closed door, and retreated to his own bedroom to consider how he next wished to meddle in Mr. Apollyon's grasp upon the object of his affections. As he made his way back the way he had come, he began to smile to himself—perhaps this time, he would merely start a childish little rumor and see what happened.

Inspired by an invitation to a party he had recently turned down because he was away from London at present, he thought Mr. Apollyon's public house might well benefit from a last-minute Halloween party. Of course, there would be no such thing, but it would be fun to see if any confusion or inconvenience would bring Alastair to him.

The man could hardly complain when nobody and nothing was harmed because of a silly little rumor.

**6**

———————

Someone, and evidently nobody knew who—apart from the detail that it was a friend of Paul's who set it all in motion—thought it would be a wonderful idea to host a Halloween party at The Queen Anne. The Apollyons were noted for their unorthodoxy, so the fact that there were no formal invitations did not seem to cause any confusion. Paul, however, was perplexed when presented with the notion.

His parents *had* hosted such parties, usually not on the day itself and also not anything so organized as to require invitations. But the taproom, foyer, and common areas would be decorated with things like tin snakes and paper skulls, and generally the light would be kept minimal. As a child, Paul had heard many ghost stories this way. The most memorable one in his estimation was probably to do with Shipden, the lost village away from shore, now submerged in the sea. Molly had echoed this tradition; the tales had their grip on local lore.

With not long to spare before the actual evening of

Halloween, Paul learned of his supposed and nebulous plans when a rather overexcited, vaguely familiar young man with brown hair and greenish eyes asked him, "What time should we arrive?"

"Arrive?" It was perfectly clear to him when people were to arrive in his pub, though it was perhaps pert to point out that one should arrive during opening hours.

"Yes, Mr. Apollyon."

Clearly, he was not privy to something the young man knew. "I should think arriving during the normal trading hours would suffice."

Miss Garland saved him as she came to the bar, looking lovely in a new dress of garnet-colored fabric that suited her dark hair. "He means your party."

"My party?" This was entirely new news to him. He did try to attend parties if invited. It depended on the person and the context, and how much he had to do, but he sometimes went. He was not known for hosting them, though. That custom had passed while his mother was still alive. She hadn't liked arranging or hosting anything quite as much as his father and grandfather, and they were more loquacious than her by far. Edward might have done more with gatherings had he stayed, and Paul reckoned he did it in Norwich if the mood struck him.

But he took more after Mother, perfectly pleased to socialize if the circumstances were present and correct, yet less likely to create them himself.

"The Halloween party," said the lad, with a bright smile. Paul then recalled his name was Daniel, but he was unaware of much past that alone.

Benson once confided that Daniel might be *that way*

inclined, or so he had heard. If so, said Benson, it was probably why he now favored The Queen Anne as he came of age to drink properly in a public house.

Paul had then asked if they were in possession of that reputation. He worried someone might take issue if The Queen Anne was known as somewhere certain criminal circumstances could be sought and procured. Of course, he did not mind at all if men like him felt comfortable under his roof. He welcomed that. But the law could be a bother when it wanted, and he didn't fancy his livelihood and home being caught in its web—especially not for reasons of attraction or love.

Benson did not believe it did, and so far, that belief had proven true. An endearing sort of strangeness was the main thing The Queen Anne was known for, shortly followed by the agreeable beers and ales. Strangeness, Paul could and did happily live with. He also didn't see a need for changing any brewing techniques or recipes if the products served everyone well enough, much like he didn't see a point in trying to refurnish and compete with any of the hotels favored by more moneyed clientele.

"The Halloween party," Paul repeated, striving for any inkling of knowledge that he had indeed set one in motion.

Miss Garland could see he was grasping at nothing; her expression quickly went from cheerful to just as confused as he was. She set her glass down on the bar and he took it without thinking, setting it out of the way of the bar's edge. "I would have thought you just announced it," she said.

Young Daniel seemed lightly distressed that Paul was not enthusiastically furnishing him with more details about the circumstances. "I heard it from Molly yesterday afternoon, who said she got it from a friend of yours."

He had been out to the bank yesterday afternoon and enjoyed the brisk walk. In that time, he didn't know who might have paid a visit, much less who would have spoken to Molly. She was generally busy in the afternoons with the hope that she could return home before it fell dark, which it did early as autumn truly descended.

Pondering which of his friends might have said such a thing, he said, "I see." While he would not say so to Daniel, he quickly concluded none of his friends would volunteer his public house for a party of any sort without asking him first.

"Oh dear," said Miss Garland, quietly and without much alarm. There had not been many spare moments within which either Alastair or Paul could speak to her about Bertie, so she did not know much about their present situation, but she did know a little about Lucas, Torquil, and the fruitless trip to Trunch.

And while she and Benson had been looking after The Queen Anne, Paul knew Benson had explained more about the reasons why they were doing so. She'd told Paul upon their return how Lucas had been perfectly honorable in paying for her services, but had been incredibly tight-lipped in general when she tried to make conversation past anything they had already said.

It made sense, she had remarked, that he would be at the root of a wild chase for nothing.

The trouble was, he wasn't at the root, not directly.

His eyes caught Alastair's across the room, thronging with people and comforting in its busy state, and whatever shone in his own, Alastair broke from his conversation with a few laborers with a smile and a laugh, and came to him immediately.

"Why do you look like you've sat upon a tack?"

"Did you tell Molly, or anybody, that you wanted to host a Halloween party here?" He didn't think so at all, but it was worth asking. In fact, he thought he knew who had first said it, even though the logic made no sense at all to him and if *he* were going to interfere with someone else's life, he would do so more directly than with dead crows and rumors of a party.

Conversely, there was seemingly no reasoning with a man who had demonstrated an almost whimsical pull to the chaotic, or what might have been called whimsical had it not been motivated more by avarice and what Paul thought was a brand of madness. He should actually term it maniacal rather than whimsical.

Alastair did not in any way seem pleased with Bertie's unpredictable behavior. But it was still taking him rather too long, in Paul's opinion, to do something about it. That Paul wanted him to do something more concrete and possibly violent was a surprise even to himself. He had not been given to such leanings before, and he was not sure if he could reconcile himself to these stirrings.

Of course, he had few concrete reasons to suspect Bertie of volunteering The Queen Anne this way, other than he had a pattern of festooning birds to the building itself like some kind of macabre bunting. That, and a low, sinking feeling in his stomach, an instinct that whispered it was correct.

He wished he could direct his abilities with purpose, cast his eye to the future and see intentionally. If anyone could do so, he did not know; all he knew was, he could not. As a child he had given it some slight experimentation and all he'd ever received for his efforts were dull, persistent headaches. If someone on the street were to ask him to predict their tomorrow, the talent was not accessible to him.

"Not at all," said Alastair. He glanced at Daniel, who blushed as Paul would've expected and done himself at that age, had someone who looked like Alastair looked at him. Then he looked with an unspoken question at Miss Garland. She shrugged. "Rather late to be announcing that, isn't it?" he said.

"Daniel, here, said Molly was told by somebody—a friend of mine—we were having a party." Paul didn't mean to make Daniel blush more than he already was, but it couldn't be helped. "Did anyone come to call while I was out?"

"No." Somehow the word was delivered slowly, a little drawn out as though it were longer than a syllable, and Paul watched Alastair arrive at the same dim conclusion he had, as unreasonable as it might have been. Though there was nothing especially harmful in starting mischief like this, one had to question the motives and the timing, and if not Bertie, then there was nobody else who presented a new variable in their lives.

It was with a tired heart that Paul smiled at Alastair, whom he didn't want to blame for anything Bertie did. He was just the connecting factor. Paul wondered, simply for a moment, if his entire life would become a bizarre game of cat and mouse with this rich fellow. They'd never even met. Bertie had just watched him.

He suppressed a shiver. *Why can't Alastair just kill him and be done with it?* The thought was intrusive, but earnest, and he hoped none of the resultant and abrupt resentment transferred into his expression. He didn't think he felt it, not truly, but it was hard to ignore once the feeling had been given words in his mind. He should be appreciative of Alastair turning over a new page; he was turning from things that could have gotten him in deep trouble and perhaps cost his life or freedom.

For all that Alastair had referenced dark acts, Paul had seen very little proof of them. Sometimes this was a source of great comfort, because Paul didn't know if he was ready to sleep alongside someone who exhibited more brutal tendencies.

Yet evidently, he might have also been comforted by the man he loved taking extreme actions to protect him. Killing Bertie would be extreme, and he didn't know if he could support one insistent, but disturbing, invasive thought that was contrary to his sense of right and wrong.

If he really listened, he might acknowledge how his sense of those things had shifted at least a little. Much as Alastair had seemingly mellowed, Paul had started to discover his teeth were sharper than he believed. He sighed and decided to parry with a little bite of his own.

He said quite calmly to Daniel, "There must have been a mistake. Perhaps Molly misunderstood. But I've heard there's to be a Halloween party at the Calders' old house, not that all of us would be invited there."

7

The early afternoon sun was deceptively bright the
next day, and Alastair drew his hat closer against
his forehead to shield his eyes. As he glanced from
left to right, he did not yet see Bertie, whose note said he
would arrive about now. They were back to the notes, now,
short things exchanged under cover of evening and with
Daniel's help, since he lived in the direction of the Calders'
old house. His grandmother had evidently known Bertie's
mother and done some char work for her, so he set off with
no hesitation as to where to go.

Daniel had seemed to feel badly, too, that he'd caused
Paul such confusion with his innocent assumption, and was
eager to go and come back with a reply. It had been a small
trick to keep this away from Paul's notice, and Alastair didn't
think it actually *was* kept from him. Paul just did not
acknowledge Daniel leaving, then coming back, despite
being neither a courier nor one who was prone to such to and
froing.

Just to be certain nobody skulked in hidden corners, Alastair crept toward the edges of the churchyard, looking into the long shadows cast by the very sunlight threatening to temporarily blind him. He supposed a faux Halloween party was better than a crow stuck to a door, but he had to question the logic of it.

Bertie came alongside him before he could get very far. "Did you think I would be lurking about?"

"To be very fair, you do have a habit of it."

Bertie's mouth shaped into a little, sly smile that Alastair had once found attractive. Now, he just didn't trust it, and the expression didn't register as much of anything at all.

"Why did you do it?"

"You shall have to be more specific."

"Tell people there was to be a party."

"Because I could." Bertie shrugged.

"Well, we aren't having one."

"It might have been good for business." There was no way to tell if he was serious; Bertie had never had to run a business or tend to anything other than his own whims. Although he was offering only an innocuous statement, nothing to do with him felt innocuous at all. "That boy you sent with your note mentioned your Mr. Apollyon said there would be a party at *my* house."

Alastair had to laugh or he would shriek. "Is that the way of it, now? You'll just keep interfering until I tell you to meet me by the church, then I'll chide you, and you'll run off to your silly house only to repeat the cycle again?" He thought for a moment that he could end this now, leaving a rich man's body in an old churchyard whose decrepit church would provide a wonderfully moody backdrop to such a murder.

Glancing at his boots, he quickly decided Bertie didn't

deserve the intimacy of his hands, and they were the only weapons he had at present. It also occurred to him that the increasingly vocal effort to repair the presently neglected St Peter and St Paul might be halted if he did something so grisly and left a body to be discovered nearby. That would be a shame.

"I've found that persistence does yield results."

Looking up to meet Bertie's eyes, he took a step closer to him. The space just behind Bertie felt charged, almost like he was being watched by a tree, but all that was beyond the churchyard was daily life: the road, shops, passersby. It wasn't precisely clandestine or even so overgrown as to be completely private. True, it was not in the best of conditions, and one needed to know where to access the churchyard itself, for the gates were ostensibly locked. One of them gave if it was pushed. Even someone like Bertie could manage to be here without attracting much notice.

Still, it was not exactly secluded during the day. Alastair had only chosen this as a meeting place because they'd met here before. Paul was well occupied with a small throng of customers who had arrived in Cromer, ironically enough, for a Halloween gathering held by a bosom friend who had no bedrooms in which to put them.

"There is no point in being persistent with me."

"So you say."

Choosing his words with care, Alastair said, "So I know, Bertie."

He was starting to suspect the only reasoning behind suddenly and haphazardly creating rumors of a party at The Queen Anne involved getting him alone. As he glared at Bertie, the hunger in Bertie's face was palpable. But it registered as different than it had been only several days ago; there seemed to be less energy behind it.

If one took into account the rather gentle nature of meddling by way of inconvenient rumors, there was less zeal in Bertie altogether, but no less desperation. He did not know what might have motivated the shift besides tiredness or Bertie's proper realization that he was the only Calder left. Alastair imagined reconciling with that, if one was rich and had property or other obligations, might be difficult.

He was the last Gow of his line, but he was under no legal responsibilities to marry for the rest of an inheritance, to maintain certain holdings, or to perform propriety.

If he were Bertie, he would make the best of what he did have and say to hell with the rest of it, but he had not been conditioned from birth to believe those matters were important. In short, it seemed to Alastair that Bertie had been both minimized as an individual yet forced to believe he would uphold specific duties should the situation demand it. But as he'd said to Lucas and Paul in various ways of late, he and Bertie had not spoken about deeper matters to do with the heart or their childhoods.

The breeze ruffled a bit of Bertie's hair that crept out from under his impeccable hat, no doubt an expensive thing that Alastair would call a Derby hat but was probably some other style.

"You look rather haunted," Alastair said. He uttered it in spite of himself. Whatever fondness there had ever been between them, it was gone for him, but he could not quite pretend it had never been there. "Like you haven't slept."

It would not be characteristic of Bertie for him to break down, to confide in Alastair. All the same, something in him appeared to falter as though he was grateful for the acknowledgement of tiredness. When Bertie did not say anything, Alastair sighed. "I hadn't thought to say this before, but...just pretend I'm dead, won't you? We are never going to come to a resolution you like."

Motionless, Bertie stared at him, the fluidity of his expression a few moments ago gone.

"You never had me, so don't pretend you did. Or do, as long as you also pretend to have lost me." Alastair waited to see if he would move or speak, and when he did not after several long seconds, Alastair turned to leave.

He resisted the temptation to end it on his own terms, still brought to heel by the thought that Bertie would enjoy dying by his hand far too much. Being arrested or even hanging in service of protecting Paul did not frighten him, but furnishing any pleasure to Bertie did.

If ever there was someone who could manage to become the most lingering and insistent ghost, it might be him, and Alastair did not want to give him even a crumb of enjoyment for fear he might try to stay for more. It was a ridiculous thought, but he could think of little else besides ghosts while he stood in a seaside churchyard dappled by late October sun.

To his disbelief, he could not hear Bertie making any moves to follow him. It was a small thing, but the lack of movement was noticeable. Time was that Bertie probably would have crept after him.

He found it curious, but was too preoccupied and happy to go back to The Queen Anne to consider what it might mean, or if it might mean anything at all.

Watching from nearby and not quite where Alastair had been looking, Lucas only relaxed after Alastair had turned his back, walked away, and a soft creak of the disused gate heralded his exit.

"You can come out from there," Bertie murmured. "I told you he wouldn't try anything against me. It's not in his nature, anymore."

Lucas was less sure about that than Bertie was. He found the urge for violence usually just hibernated, and one only got better at using violent behavior more judiciously. He didn't know if it truly left, though he had to admit his own behavior had become more sedate over the years. It felt like he could be more intentional with his choices regarding violence, at the very least, and it seemed Alastair had reached a similar point where viciousness did not need to be a primary option, as it had been when they were coming up together.

Some of his own propensity for thoughtless violence had ebbed away once he'd saved up enough to leave Old Ross's lodgings, and it was no longer encouraged by his caretaker's temperament and actions. Fortunately, the man had never been any kind of boss with a group of child miscreants. Lucas had been allowed to leave because there was no manipulation of that sort between him and his dubious guardian, but it was also made clear to him that he had nowhere to return should things turn dire.

There was some vague connection between Ross and his mother, whom he could not remember. From what he had been told as a boy, Ross was his uncle, but the relation sometimes changed to that of a cousin. He hadn't thought Ross was secretly his father, for there was no resemblance between them. One of them had frightfully red hair; the other a dusty brown that might have always been closer to gray even in youth. Though alcoholism had rendered Ross's nose spread and perpetually pink and mottled with veins, even apart from that, their faces looked completely unalike.

Old enough now to understand the difference might signify nothing, and they might well have been related as father and son, he'd simply decided not to give it much more thought at all.

It didn't matter what he had been. Old Ross was dead and there'd been nothing left to Lucas, or around for him to claim. Creditors and bailiffs had come to strip the little tenement of anything of value, with anything else being scavenged by the sort of people who seemed to make it their business to skulk around where there were recently deceased and see what was left.

He was informed of this by a former neighbor, a chandler who didn't seem sorry to see the back of Ross. Nobody was.

Face upturned to the sky as he assessed the few clouds, Lucas said, "And I told *you* that prank was a soft one. Why bother?" He had said so in the brief moment when Bertie had mentioned sending someone out with the supposed knowledge that Mr. Apollyon's pub was to be the site of a party.

It was jejune, really, and Lucas could not see the point of it at all. As with the chase Bertie had set him and Torquil upon, the journey down here to find Alastair and press him into a quest for misplaced smugglers' gains, Lucas knew Bertie liked to see what people would do if presented with certain factors and influences. He suspected it was little more than that, for Bertie seemed tired. He was almost going about life as a child sometimes did if they needed a rest, and could not have one.

"Well, he came to see me over it," said Bertie.

Lucas did not want that to hurt, but it did. Because he was growing used to the hurt and Bertie seemed more resigned to Alastair's lack of cooperation than galvanized by it, he just let it sting. With luck, it might be that things were shifting in Bertie's head to be in his favor.

Unfortunately for his pride and against his better judgement, he was happy being near Bertie. He might never be as happy as Alastair seemed with his Mr. Apollyon. Even mere days around them demonstrated a contentedness he was not sure he could reach himself. But given his past, he was willing to reassess what happiness meant and how it might be for him.

"To tell you to pretend he was dead."

"Do you think he meant it?"

It was not a question Lucas thought he would hear; the sentiment rang obviously enough to him, and he'd been standing almost far enough away not to catch the words. He had, but someone with less excellent hearing might not have. "Do you want me to lie, or tell you the truth?"

Close enough to Bertie to touch him or embrace him, Lucas refrained from doing either. He had no doubt this space might be used for such clandestine matters, but the fact remained that it was quite in the middle of things for somewhere so disused. He kept his hands at his sides.

Still, Bertie did take half a step closer to him. Hardly daring to be encouraged by the movement, Lucas held his tongue.

"Truth," said Bertie.

"He wants you to leave him alone. You scared him too much for there ever to be anything between you, any friendship."

Lucas had seen what Alastair feared, and Bertie had gone for the heart of it. The crows had frightened Alastair because they reminded him of a life he had seemingly stepped away from, but more crucially, they were festooned to his lover's public house, which had by all appearances become a sanctum. Bertie had shattered the peace, the illusion that old choices and friends could not reach him in Cromer.

He was not poetic enough himself to be able to think of his own heart existing in others, in their souls or emotions or whatever force of life animated bodies. Still, he'd heard about it in songs and stories, and having eavesdropped upon a great many conversations, it seemed a real experience that was denied him. It was just as well; he'd always had enough of a mess on his own without accounting for anybody else.

Of course, until Lucas had come himself and seen the sort of life Alastair was living, he could not have advised Bertie on how to proceed. When Bertie had sat in The Sow and relayed old tales about his relations' criminal mishaps and how Lucas might benefit from them—and exact a little revenge upon Alastair through inconvenience and menace— he did not know his former associate had found himself in love.

He might still have proceeded in his own endeavors, for the lure of both money and creating annoyance for Alastair were persuasive. But if he had seen how Alastair looked at Mr. Apollyon, he would have told Bertie not to foster any hopes to reunite with Alastair at all.

He huffed and returned his eyes to Bertie. There was only so long one could study the sky by way of distraction.

If he wasn't careful, he would find himself in that same lovesick state and his heart would be wandering around without him, likely in a fine house in Cromer or London or Edinburgh with a wife on its arm, and him passing lonely evenings in an empty bed. Expecting Bertie to have made a tart reply to the pronouncement that Alastair wished to be left alone by now, Lucas was unnerved by his silence.

While he'd been musing on clouds, Bertie's eyes had gone wide and unseeing. Though the world around him continued to move, the breeze rustling leaves and murmurs carrying into the churchyard, he stood utterly motionless. Concerned, for Lucas hadn't seen such a thing from Bertie and didn't believe it was feigned, he took a tentative step closer to him.

**8**

———

Of all the places, Bertie was outside at night by the old duckpond opposite his house in Cromer. It was a lovely pond, somewhere he'd often snuck off to as a child to try having a moment alone—generally after he had shaken off whatever awful compound Michael had slipped into his tea that particular afternoon, and sometimes while he still experienced odd effects like shimmering, glittering horizons.

In addition, the pond was larger than one might have expected, even if it wasn't quite big enough to feature anything ornamental, such as a faux classical temple in the middle, or statues along its edges. A small outbuilding stood to one side, always a pretty sight. The night was cold and clear, and smelled green, like damp grass.

Bertie took a breath, knowing he was in a vision and somewhat comforted he was having one like this. They had been sparse ever since he had inherited, much like those that visited him through dreams had been sporadic since he had reached Cromer. Brushing thoughts of Michael from his mind like excess dust from an old cellar shelf, he watched the outbuilding, where his attention had been drawn.

Presently, the door flew open. With eagerness, he waited to see who came out. It was himself, which was interesting: as a child, there had been more visions like this one where he watched like an onlooker at a play, but they'd grown fewer as he grew older.

He dragged something behind him, large and unwieldy. An old chair of the sort a groundskeeper might keep in a weathered outbuilding, with a person attached to it. Frowning, Bertie tried to make out who sat there, but it was difficult without the person facing him. It was a man, or someone in trousers and a shirt, topped with a nondescript hat.

The frown melted into a smile. Not just any man, but Mr. Apollyon, he saw, as the vision's Bertie maneuvered him closer to the edge of the pond.

However, where there should have been excitement in his heart, he found a disconcerting amount of dread. The version of himself he watched from the outside did not seem happy or triumphant, either, as he hauled an evidently bound Mr. Apollyon on the chair to the water and tipped him in.

It was not more than several moments later that he felt a hand on his shoulder, but when he turned to see who touched him, nobody was there to match the unseen hand.

"Bertie?"

He blinked and the vision went blurry as though appearing through heavy rain, though the night's scents and sounds had not changed.

Lucas was no expert or medical man, but he thought Bertie might be having some kind of fit. He didn't want to move him or startle him, but couldn't think that leaving him precisely where he was would be healthy. The best he could think to do was say his name and rest a palm on his shoulder.

Motionless, eyes open, Bertie stood there gazing out at who knew what, leaving Lucas to stare at him unhelpfully for almost a minute. His pupils were the correct size; Lucas had known men whose pupils went funny or mismatched after blows to the head, so he only assumed the same thing could happen in other situations. It had never heralded good things, so he was relieved Bertie's were normal.

He was contemplating carrying Bertie off and summoning a doctor once they were situated in his beautiful old house, until Bertie blinked and gave a great shudder. He stared at Lucas and said, "How long has it been?"

"Not more than a minute," said Lucas, who was relieved, but still wanted to shout at him for the fright.

"They're always funny that way."

He must have meant the fits. Perhaps he had suffered from them all along, the entire time he had known Lucas, and they were normal to him.

For an outsider, they appeared daunting. "Have these always happened to you?"

"Oh," said Bertie, and he looked around without moving his head, like he ascertained his surroundings or tried to remind himself of where he had been. "Yes."

"They must not be terribly frequent. Never seen you like that, before."

Working his mouth a little, Bertie looked around at him

and smiled almost softly. "You're correct. These specific ones are not so frequent. They happen more at night."

"Thank fuck for that."

"What did it look like?"

"Like you were there and not there. You went so still, but your eyes were open." He nodded to one of the forgotten and unkempt benches nearby. "Let's sit for a spell before you try to go home. Besides, I don't trust that Alastair has gone directly home, if that was where he was headed after meeting you."

He'd never seen anybody with such an affliction, so he didn't know precisely what to do. To his surprise, Bertie allowed himself to be gently shepherded to the bench. He did not tremble and didn't seem weak, but he went along with Lucas's arm about his waist, and sat readily.

"You're the first to have seen me that way," said Bertie, "first that I know of, anyway."

The words brought a ridiculous amount of pride, or pleasure, that he had been the only one to see Bertie so vulnerable. Then he said, taking back his own arm once Bertie had settled and he sat next to him, "I'm sure somebody must have seen you."

"I don't think so. I've worked very hard to keep them from others."

"Is that possible?" Knowing as little as he did, Lucas assumed the process couldn't be controlled at all, and keeping such a clear leave of one's senses secret seemed an impossible task. Enough to drive one a little erratic and strange. He thought of how Bertie now seemed more imperious, and more fickle, and would have asked him directly if these episodes were grating on him. Perhaps between his brother's death, even though there was no love lost between them, and this personal circumstance, things were getting to be a little too much.

"More or less," said Bertie, chuckling weakly. "I mean to say, I don't know for sure, but I think mental discipline can keep them at bay, or at least make them take other forms. Dreams, mostly."

It sounded mad, and Lucas said so. "I don't know if you can bend fits to your will."

When quiet stretched between them, or as much quiet as there could be amidst a working day with people going about their routines even as they lingered in a neglected space, Lucas suspected Bertie would not answer him.

The lack of a response would have been understandable or expected, for in spite of coming to know each other carnally and developing more of a tender rapport of late, there were years of a charged friendship to contend with. In his experience, Bertie had only told him things when it suited him, and Lucas hadn't much cared, attributing it to their different places in life and temperamental preferences in general.

Bertie was not the sort who wanted to seem weak to anybody, and especially not anybody he regarded as his social inferiors, even if they were his friend. So Lucas waited and watched the changing sunlight dapple the poor, old church.

"They're not fits."

It wasn't what he expected Bertie to say at all. "Looked that way to me."

He had also heard of headaches that could incapacitate a person. Torquil's mother, evidently, had suffered from them throughout his life and until the end of her own. She would be going about her day and be struck by pain so badly, it might stop her almost exactly where she stood. Torquil had said it was the sort of thing where all one could do to help was guide her to bed, and without money for continued visits to a proper doctor, they'd made do with rest being the remedy.

"I can tell you what they are, if you promise not to think me mad."

"I already do." A gentle joke only, somewhat true, but not meant to hurt Bertie. When a soft chuckle met his ears, he smiled.

"Fair enough. I might be, but not for this." He looked at Lucas, and Lucas might have forgotten everything but the blue Bertie looked with. "They're not fits. I have visions. Premonitions, you could say, of the future."

## 9

———

"Fuck off."

To be fair, Bertie was not sure why he had said it at all; he had not told anybody, and he had not thought it through now. It had even slipped out with serenity, though now that he had spoken, a cavalcade of nerves had descended upon him. How was he to explain the tricky nature of the visions? Their rather odd way of showing him versions of a future? He hadn't been wrong, before, but he *had* seen multiple ways something might happen, or things that later turned out to be more metaphorical than literal.

Sometimes it was not even of much help at all. He had not been presented with any of Michael's diabolical pranks, none of the many instances when his tea was doctored with an opiate or another chemical that infiltrated his mind and might linger. None of the times he'd been served something seemingly innocent, a bit of cake or a sweet, disguising something similar. None of the moments when he was pricked with a dart that had been dipped in substances meant to see him take leave of his senses.

Michael *was* clever, but neither Mother nor Father would have really noticed, spending as little time with Bertie as they did. At times they might pass a remark on how pale he seemed, but that was it. They hadn't known he'd suffered at Michael's hand.

If they couldn't warn him, what was the visions' use?

For anyone who was not him or in possession of the same type of ability, he believed the concept itself might be a challenge, never mind the nuances and caveats. With trepidation, he waited for Lucas's expression to settle as it showed consternation, almost anger, then cautious resignation.

Why Lucas was to be privy to this secret of his, he didn't know. Then again, he'd turned to his bed with the intention of keeping him compliant and slaking his own agitated lust. Yet their relations brought them both pleasure and they kept seeking each other. If he had to be truthful, there was not just pleasure, there was solace, and it motivated him. He had to suspect Lucas felt something of the same.

Or, he was just enjoying himself. *Alastair just enjoyed himself.* The thought brought with it spite.

"I'm in earnest."

"I can see *you* believe what you're saying." Lucas' eyes didn't waver from his, though Bertie could tell he sorted through several thoughts at once. He often downplayed his own intelligence, claiming others were smarter than him and implying his role was better if it didn't involve making large decisions. But years of being around Lucas even just sporadically had shown Bertie that was not entirely true. He might prefer for others to decide and direct things, but he was not without the means to do so himself if he chose.

At present, he was most likely sorting through their

shared memories for a scrap of evidence to support what Bertie said. Not wide and unseeing eyes, as Bertie did believe the amount of mental fortitude he devoted to appearing ordinary did work—nobody in his life had ever remarked upon his fits, or strange headaches, or any marked and repeated inattentiveness.

They had not seen them. And if they had, they might look very much like quotidian maladies.

But Lucas would know to look for other tells. Finally, he said, "The first time you spoke to me." Bertie had mentioned the blue quilt and asked about the bruises on his face. "The *second* time you spoke to me."

Bertie remembered the second time well, too. The slender butcher's boy had come a few days after their first meeting with another order, this time a smaller one, something special for an intimate and last-minute dinner his father had decided to host for a pair of colleagues, two local physicians whom he wished to make good with. Bertie had been waiting for Lucas with an umbrella because it was raining heavily, and though Lucas was already soaked through, Bertie used the umbrella to walk him back to the servants' door.

"Yes?"

"You had no reason to wait for me with an umbrella. Your housekeeper or cook might have known when I was to come, but why would you?"

"They could have told me you were coming."

"Did they?"

"No." Bertie reached over and held his hand, briefly, before letting it settle back on the bench. "I dreamt of you coming that afternoon, the night before. I don't know why I knew the time, or even the day..." he sighed. "Knowing why isn't often accessible to me."

He had attempted many times to understand with logic how his abilities worked, but with the only resources available to him being books of fairy tales and folklore, or overly didactic Christian tracts, logic was thin on the ground. It was possible only to know nebulously and instinctively, not always precisely. "But I knew you'd be there, I knew it would be raining so much, and I went to wait for you."

"It's always wet in Edinburgh." Lucas would know, being from Old Town.

"But you were not always waiting to be let into the servants' door."

With a sigh of his own, Lucas said, "This dream... you just... *saw* me. What, as I was? Soaked to the bone, trying to protect the shit I had to deliver lest I be *beaten* to the bone?"

When someone said it aloud, it did sound absurd. "Yes."

"And before then, you knew about my room, the bruises that would be on my face..." Lucas took a breath. "Even... almost the first moment you spoke to me."

"That one was only a flash," said Bertie, studying his own shoes.

"Christ, what else do you see?"

His mouth working soundlessly for a moment, Bertie did not know what to say. "Surprisingly mundane things." He could not know if this was because one of his family's greatest values was order, so he was conditioned to see more banal than extraordinary things, or if anybody who might see the future was also privy to ordinary knowledge. Then he thought of what he had just seen himself doing to Mr. Apollyon and it brought him a strange sense of resolution. "Sometimes, less mundane things." It had to be said, he did not often see horrific ones or violent ones. He did not know what he was going to do to Michael until he had done it.

*Perhaps the universe is bringing you some new directions.* It may well be that he was not meant to be with Alastair. Perhaps what he had seen of Alastair in his Cromer house were dregs of a future that no longer existed, or things were always in flux anyway, or his mind was merely trying to give him what he wanted. Who wouldn't want to experience him in bed murmuring endearments and promises of always? From what Bertie had experienced in reality, these flashes looked and felt postcoital, though Alastair had not made mention of *always* or *forever* in those cases.

He did not have answers to these points, and it felt good to believe this was what he would be given in the future—or by the future. If Mr. Apollyon's death was the thing to unlock it, that could be an acceptable price. Or even if it would not give him Alastair, it would give him closure of a sort.

He was already a murderer, was he not? What was one more person added to his brother? Bertie felt there might be ways to extricate Mr. Apollyon's body from the chair after the fact, and then it could all look like an accident. His surname was not one of old money or an aristocratic family. But he did command a small fortune. And even if Michael had not been able to equal Father in matters of esteem and respect, friends of the family could attest to Bertie's good character, as could Bertie's solicitor.

As a voice within him attested he did not want to be so wicked, not really, he placated it by saying this would be the last time he'd indulge. Then he could move forward, away from Alastair, but without letting Alastair have any rewards for having taken him for granted.

For all Alastair's experience with hardship and wickedness, Bertie was resentful he'd seemed to shed both like they were naught but delicate shawls. He felt destined to wear them more often than most would.

IF HE HAD WANTED a husband who told him everything and did not insist upon slipping outside under duress, he should not have pinned all his hopes on Alastair Gow, who made a habit of it. Paul watched as Alastair made his way back inside after having been out for over an hour.

The sun was setting as he came inside The Queen Anne, his clothes rumpled by the breeze and likely his own fidgeting. A steady flow of customers was present in the taproom, which meant Paul could not intercept him as easily as he would have preferred. Rather brazen, Alastair caught his eye, smiled ruefully, and ambled toward Benson's corner. It was a pretense only, Paul was sure, and Alastair just did not want to talk to him yet.

Benson wouldn't wait for Alastair to talk.

Paul would almost bet there had been another discussion with Bertie. About what, he couldn't say. While he trusted Alastair not to succumb to any pressure Bertie applied, he resented the continued intrusion into their life and had no desire for this to last until Bertie tired of it, got married, found some other man to harass, or died.

Death might be the simplest option of those.

He knew he should be proud that Alastair had not gone

to that extreme, but he wasn't. Something nagged at him, and it was barely formed around the edges, a dull sense of urgency and danger wrought by the sheer ambiguity of the situation. Bertie had not marched into his public house and confronted him; there had been no overt declarations of anything at all.

Paul was dueling with a shadow he had not even seen, while Alastair enacted a newfound sense of mercy against it. That was worthy of respect, yet Paul could not sit idly by and trust all would come out all right. The shadow was agitated and intent for reasons only it knew, and Paul was of the opinion that Alastair was not the cause so much as whatever ideal image of him the shadow had latched onto.

Perhaps Bertie had found security within his attachment to Alastair, such as it was, and still scrambled for it now that his old life had changed so much. Circumstances could close in upon someone until they did not recognize the harm done, and since he had been kept from meeting Bertie, he could not say for himself what he thought the trouble was.

It was possibly for the best that he hadn't, and he did appreciate that Bertie stayed away—at least from him— because the urge to be aggressive was starting to take hold where civility and curiosity might have won otherwise.

The evening passed remarkably quickly because he was so lost in his own thoughts. He knew he interacted with people, yet would be pressed to recall anything he said or what they drank.

"I'm sorry," said Alastair, hours later, as they both dressed for bed.

Too cold to sleep naked, Paul was pulling a nightshirt over his head. "For what?"

"Melting away like I do, and—"

"You went to talk to him about the party business." Paul had assumed things would have just fettered out if people arrived on Halloween and discovered it was only another night, perhaps with more candles and a few decorations if he could be bothered to dig them out. Of the things Bertie had put in motion, this one was more of a joke.

Even though Alastair had unburdened himself of what Paul hoped were the last major secrets in his life, clearly, the habit of making clandestine moves was as well-worn as his pair of boots. Paul sighed and added, "I don't expect you to change overnight. I know it was hard to tell me about James and Evie, and I can tell it's hard for you to think about a time before we met."

In a way, that was a beautiful thing. Paul was prepared to see it as such once Bertie had been more properly dealt with. He liked how Alastair's sense of true north had recalibrated to be here; he only wanted more forthrightness, as he had for weeks and even months. It was not something he would castigate Alastair for, but it was a lie to say he wasn't frustrated by Alastair's disinclination to be vulnerable.

"Well, to be fair to you, James isn't the one wreaking havoc on your nerves."

Choosing what he asked next carefully and going to the washbasin to splash a bit of water on his face, Paul murmured, "Are you protecting him, or me?" He didn't mean James. And he did not think there were any lingering romantic feelings for Bertie, but he wished to know why the evasiveness felt necessary to Alastair.

"Always you," said Alastair, without a hint of annoyance or defensiveness.

"But?"

The bed creaked softly under Alastair's weight as he sat down. Paul did not need to see to know he'd taken a seat, and he patted his face dry before turning to Alastair.

"I know it sounds ridiculous, but whatever is wrong with him...I don't think I'm at the root of it at all."

"Which is why you can tolerate so much from him." Paul had no intent to sound as bitter as he did, and even in the low candlelight, Alastair appeared pained to catch the bitterness in his tone.

"I suppose so."

By way of apology, Paul went to his side of the bed and got under the covers, rolling to his side and facing Alastair. He rested his hand on Alastair's upper thigh, warm under the fabric of his shirt. He'd stopped undressing after removing his boots, socks, and trousers, seemingly distracted by his own thoughts, for Paul had not said a word before he stopped. The first thing Alastair had said once they'd made it upstairs was, *I'm sorry.*

"If you let me meet him, arranged a meeting, I mean, I might be able to help you determine what's actually wrong."

"Is that what you would have me do?" Peering at him, Alastair did sound as though he asked with earnestness. "Somehow, I think him seeing you in the flesh and not just behind your own windows might send him deeper into whatever spiral he's in."

First, the reminder that Bertie had indeed spied upon them through The Queen Anne's windows brought some rage. Then Paul answered the question. "I *would* have you kill him for his trouble..."

Surprise only evident in his eyes, his face otherwise still, Alastair said, "Truly?"

"Yes." In this, Paul did not waver. "But it would be too much of a mess with the law." He toyed with the hem of Alastair's shirt, sneaking his fingers under it and petting skin instead of cotton. "I know he's the only one left of his family, and I'm sure he has friends and connections. Someone would know he was gone. And I think it could be connected to you or us, if you did it. Perhaps not immediately, but eventually."

The rage grew when Paul reflected and realized he actually did not know what Bertie's people had even done to get their money, or what he did, or anything about him other than he was flitting into Alastair's life, as though insisting upon them being together was as casual as popping into a milliner's shop for a new hat or walking along the prom and then to the beach.

At length, he said quietly, "I have to know if you're protecting me out of shame or love. Right now, I can't make up my mind as to which, and I don't want it to be shame."

This, apparently, Alastair would not bear with docility. In almost a moment, he had Paul pinned under him with his forearms on either side of Paul's head.

Even though the counterpane and sheets separated their bodies, it was thrilling all the same.

"I *have* learned my lesson about shame, so it isn't that." Alastair wet his lips with the edge of his tongue, then said with a smile, "If you want to know, I worry I may lose my head and do him a violence more each time I see him. It's infuriating that he should come here and make demands of me. Scare you." He chuckled with little mirth. "Scare me. Coerce a friend from the past into antagonizing me."

"Why don't you?" Paul blinked up at him.

"If I am to fall back into old habits, I don't want it to be *him* who forces my hand."

"And if I asked you?"

"You wouldn't," said Alastair. He pressed a kiss to Paul's forehead. "At least, you're *not* asking me."

Not so very long ago at all, Paul had wondered if it might make him boring, but Alastair did appear to like the quality. "Make no mistake, it's not because I value his life."

"Why, then?"

"I value yours."

Puzzlement drifted into Alastair's words. "How do you mean?"

"I wouldn't be parted from you. If I asked you to kill for me, you might well be locked away. Or transported. Hanged, far more likely. It's selfish, I suppose, but in a way, I would resent Bertie even more if his dying led to your end."

That brought laughter, not loud guffaws, but unbridled, quiet chuckles. Under Alastair as Paul was, he relished feeling them. "Sometimes, I *really* think you did miss your calling as a wickedly cool fence, or someone who should have been in charge of me when I was wilder."

"What makes you think I'm not in charge of you now?" To emphasize both the question and the sentiment, Paul arched up and met Alastair's lips with his own.

Alastair kissed him readily and warmly. "Incredibly fair thing to say. It's just as well you are, for I'm far better with you than without you."

**10**
———

Benson stood before him in the back parlor facing the sea, presently kitted out with a large carpetbag and an enormous satchel strewn over his shoulder. He looked like nothing so much as an itinerant man from myths, who could either curse or bless someone, depending upon his whim. "That should be everything, Benson, but if there is something I've missed, I'm sure we can arrange a better visit. Now just isn't a convenient time for me to go," said Paul.

Edward's old trunk couldn't be managed by one person or perhaps even two, and decidedly not without a cart of some type. Paul didn't care about his brother's belongings being returned to him so much as Benson seemed to need a purpose and a bit of a journey. In addition, Paul felt it might be better for him to be elsewhere for the moment.

What Benson carried was only a fraction of what Edward had mentioned in his letter as being in the trunk. As both brothers were busy with their respective businesses, and in the case of one of them, a new addition to the family who could not contribute anything at all to his own upkeep, Paul met Edward partway and picked through for the things he felt would bring the most joy.

Among these were some soft toys and a handful of children's books that could be read to the very young and newest Apollyon, these previously having belonged to both Paul and Edward. Their main topic were fairy tales, and Paul couldn't imagine the books being of no interest for bedtime stories.

But the primary reason for sending any of this with Benson, rather than go himself, was precisely to give Benson something to do besides be underfoot. Paul had not had any sort of premonition indicating that Benson would come to harm, but he did feel that *something* was coming to a head. The trouble was, however, that he could not tell what it was.

Indeed, if Bertie simply kept annoying him by starting odd little rumors about parties, it might simply be inconveniences upon inconveniences that made him lose his temper.

Though fiction might lead all to believe otherwise, it seemed even danger could be absurdly straightforward, or at least people who might pose a danger were still subject to human whims. Bertie did seem prone to the same kinds of caprice as anybody. Benson's magic could be thanked for protecting the premises, but there was no telling what would happen if a talented, mysterious witch with a reliance upon drink would do if some rich interloper crossed him.

"You just want me well away."

Paul had the grace to sigh and glance at the floor, to the rug under his feet. "It isn't that I want you away forever, and more that I think there might be something about to happen."

"Why not just have me stay, then?"

It was difficult to put into words, and Paul thought merely

that it was simpler to have fewer people he cared about under the roof that had been the subject of Bertie's interest. The man felt, to him, like a static charge, unseen but likely to cause a spark if any contact was made. "I just have a sense that it will be better to have you out of the way."

"He is more than he seems."

"How so?"

"Not certain, my lad, but whatever he is, it has festered. Or maybe atrophied."

Considering this, Paul said, "Can that happen?"

"If a talent is shoved to one side, so to speak?" Benson nodded gently and resettled his grip on his bag. "I believe so."

"I don't want to believe he has any type of ability beyond a large amount of money at his disposal."

"It would scare you if he were anything but ordinary?"

If Paul considered the details, Bertie was not an interloper. He was from Norfolk. Maybe not Cromer itself, but certainly the county. At times, he felt like he was doing war with some version of himself. That the man was unreadable —as the wealthy were often raised to be with their intentions and emotions—and suffered from some brand of instability, was not in question. Were he anyone else, Paul might venture a guess at there being magic at play, but Bertie did not seem to have an eccentric streak in his person, and from Paul's perspective, one needed some bit of eccentricity to be magical.

"Is it that obvious?" Paul asked, after a few moments had run away from him while he tried to make sense of Bertie and his doings.

He suspected there could be no making sense of them, but it was in his nature to try anyway. Whether through empathy, intuition, or logic, he found he could make sense of the majority of things in his own way. The trouble was, it did not always match with others' definition of sense.

"Only if somebody knows you."

"Well, I shall miss you."

"Of course," said Benson. "But if I'm well away in Norwich delivering bits and bobs to your brother, and saying hello to mine, whatever mess you two get yourselves into with that supercilious blond lad will be your own."

He let slip a chuckle at the description of Bertie being a *supercilious blond lad*. "Will your charms hold?"

"Are you worried?"

"You *just* said there would be a mess."

"They'll hold, but they're on the building, not upon you. Charms on a person are too tricky, unless you're charming yourself."

Crinkling his nose and dismissing the idea of lacking protection himself, Paul shook his head. "I don't plan on courting trouble."

"No," said Benson, as he walked past Paul with more noise than usual when Edward's various belongings clattered gently together, "you aren't courting it; you married it."

For a full span of at least half a minute, Paul watched Benson's retreating back and listened as he trundled down the stairs to the ground floor. He mentally conceded this was true.

Then he hurried after him. "Tell Edward we do well." He had already written, in brief, about himself and Alastair, owning to nothing overtly because that never seemed wise to put in writing, unless it was meant to go to Alastair himself. All the same, he was sure Edward would understand. There had never been any misunderstanding or repulsion between them on the subject of Paul's affections.

"I shall."

Edward had been out of The Queen Anne more than Paul in the couple of years before he had married, so he had not come to know Benson as well. There was a camaraderie between them all the same. Paul could trust Benson to relay not only material things, but also messages, to Edward.

He wasn't sure why he had not dispatched him to do so before, as Benson so often went to call upon his own brother and had, until very recently, split his living accommodations between said brother's house on Magdalen Street in Norwich and The Queen Anne.

Now he resided here, but confirmed he would keep the habit of visiting Timothy. Or Timmy, as Benson called him, in spite of a preference to be addressed by his full name.

"Safe travels," Paul said, just as Benson headed for the front door.

His answer was a jaunty wave of a hand, a couple of Benson's old silver rings catching the morning light as Paul caught the back of it.

He smiled to himself, and was about to make his way to the kitchen when a pair of very strong arms clasped him about the waist and brought him closer to an equally strong torso. His smile widened. "I trust nobody is downstairs."

Even *they* did not cavort when there might be a chance of anyone seeing them. There had been quick, warm kisses, but nothing that induced more than heavy breathing and a quivering sense of longing for the privacy of the landlord's flat, or their reclaimed back parlor. And the cellar, if absconding there proved more convenient than going up some stairs.

Four times now, they *had* gotten up to rather a lot in the cellar. Thankfully, its walls could be more easily cleaned than linens and bedsheets, which had been somewhat surprising to discover.

"Not that I've seen. Molly and that lad she recommended for the window washing must be underfoot, though I haven't yet said good morning to either of them." Alastair squeezed his waist and held him closer.

Paul glanced over his shoulder, though he couldn't quite see Alastair's face due to how he was being held. "Back parlor?"

"Back parlor."

IF THERE WAS SOMEWHERE BETTER than this, even in anyone's ideas of heaven, Alastair still did not want to see it. Regardless, the manner in which light splashed the room made it look like a painting, all the deceptive warmth from the sun touching the old furnishings and solid crossbeams already patinaed by tobacco smoke. In truth, it was not so warm; this was autumn sunlight and could only be trusted for illumination, even if that illumination had a golden cast when the clouds allowed for it.

He appreciated it for how it brought out flickers of auburn in Paul's dark hair, and reached down to pet it idly.

Paul said, "I don't think we should do that on the table, again. I thought it was going to crack, not that I cared."

Alastair glanced over his head and considered the table in question. It looked old, but almost everything in The Queen Anne had been inherited or scavenged from somewhere, so it probably was. If he had his guess, it dated from around the Reformation, which would have made it antique.

How disrespectful they'd been to it.

At present, they were on a wide chaise longue a customer had offered to Paul after clearing out her late mother's home, and since he'd liked the puce upholstery, he'd bought it off her for a song. As a consequence of the lack of proper planning, their parlor was looking mismatched with its possibly Reformation-era table, the sofa that had been here already, and now the chaise longue, but Alastair rather enjoyed it that way.

Besides, the best feature was the wide window overlooking the sea, and he imagined little would overshadow that besides what they often did in the back parlor.

"We don't have to ruin the old thing," he said. "It's pretty." He grinned and stroked the side of Paul's neck. "But if we did, we could always find another one."

He heard the mirrored smile in Paul's voice. "I've been meaning to ask..."

Since they had already recently discussed almost everything Alastair was afraid to, from his son to how he had managed to have such an income allowing for the son to be sent money, Alastair said, "Go ahead. Wait, did you lock the door?" He thought so, but could not quite recall. Neither of them was in a state of full undress, but things were untucked and unbuttoned, and hair was wildly mussed.

"Yes. The key is still in it." Paul paused. "You *do* remember mentioning that knotwork..."

"From Japan?" Alastair's grin widened. He thought he knew what was coming. Paul made reference to a venerable artform used by monks in pursuit of meditation, and had seemingly also been used for erotic purposes by those who had not espoused celibacy.

Alastair had found it in a book some years ago and the idea had never quite left him. He'd just never had a partner whom he would trust with such an exercise, much less whom he would want to be tied up by or with. Neither would he want any of them to be tied up around him. Most of the time, he had either to leave, or for them to leave as quickly as possible after certain needs were met. But he'd practiced some of the diagrams of knots on himself, chosen from the ones it was possible to self-administer.

Some weeks ago, he had spoken of all of this to Paul, who had remained quiet on the subject itself and moved on to asking if he had checked one of the kegs. But Alastair knew better than to assume quietness was dismissal. And he had not made mention with any particular aim.

He had simply remembered being interested, and brought it up that same evening; the association had been prompted by a fisherman who'd stopped in earlier, then taken his beer to sit in the corner with a length of thin twine. He'd silently knotted his way through his drinking, and it had summoned to Alastair's mind both pleasurable knotwork and the sailor's art of scrimshaw.

The way the ropes had been drawn in the book he'd seen reminded him greatly of intricate carvings, only instead of ivory, wood, or teeth being the canvas, the body served that purpose.

"Yes, that," said Paul. "I would try it with you. We could go beyond...being tied to the bedposts."

"Anything in particular that's brought this about?"

"I'm not competing with Bertie, that's for certain. He looks like the sort of person who would pale at any mention of being tied up in pursuit of pleasure."

There was no world in which Alastair would not laugh at either the words or their tone. He also did suspect Paul was trying to compete, if only a little, not that he needed to at all. "You do have the measure of him. But I never spoke to him about it, to be fair."

"Would you have wanted to?"

"Not in the slightest. If you want the truth of it, whenever he stayed the night, I felt like something of a stranger in my own bed."

"Did you ever stay in his?"

Sighing, for he did not especially enjoy thinking back to that time, he said, "Not more than he was in mine." He had no wish to explain the intricacies of logistics, or why certain choices had been made over others. "I can find some silk rope."

"What about scarves?"

"If you just want to be tied to the bedposts, we can keep using the longer scarves or neckties. If you want to be made a painting of knots, we'll need something longer," said Alastair, still petting his neck to savor the softness of his skin. "I *can* tie you to the bedposts without delay, though. We would have to choose an opportune time when you're not needed for something else, but scarves and ties aren't in short supply."

"Wouldn't you let me go if I needed to work? Sometimes people want the landlord and no one else will do."

"Absolutely not," Alastair replied, and his smile was back, "not until you'd reached completion at least twice."

A shiver went through Paul, and Alastair holding him as he was, felt it with desire. "Understood. And I'd like to be so bold as to demand a third, though I may regret it in the moment. I could hardly stand after the last time, and that was only once."

Yes, nothing in the hereafter could possibly compare to this, to the feel of his husband in his arms and the sound of his voice coursing through his chest as much as it did through the air, tempting him to imagine a whole course of earthly delights.

## 11

Not for the first time in his life, Bertie decided he felt segmented from his powers, if one could call them that, or that they controlled him more than he could bid them. Other times like this had coincided with, oddly enough, the usual growth spurts a boy experienced, or stress, but he was neither a boy, nor would he say he was under stress at present.

Others might disagree. Perhaps he could not call circumstances stressful for fear of what that might mean for him. But on the whole, he considered himself motivated rather than pressed upon. The main sources of tension were Alastair's reticence and his devotion to Mr. Apollyon, neither of which were particularly directed at Bertie.

Not the way Michael had directed things at Bertie, or how the occasional Eaton bully had directed things at him. Bertie brushed those associations aside as he squirmed to get more comfortable in bed.

The only waking vision he'd had for weeks had been the one of Mr. Apollyon and the duckpond, while the dreams had proved slippery. Whatever phase he was experiencing, he did not like it, for prior to now, he found things had always reconciled themselves and gone back to the predictably unpredictable when it came to his foresight.

He sighed and focused on the wall of his bedroom, which like many bedrooms in an old house, bore hairline cracks in the plaster. He thought them charming; he had studied Classics at Cambridge, a course of action that Michael deemed a mere pastime. He had said worse. Done much worse.

This time of separation from more than a few scattered visions felt keener than the others, but then, he was older. Perhaps it was age. It might have been all the interference of change. Even though it was a good thing he now had most of the resources he had never really expected to, it was a different existence than the one he'd had several months ago. He also now understood that, as the heir, he had to meet certain requirements to access some of Father's money.

While this had applied to Michael, too, Bertie could not help but wonder if it was more directed at him. He felt his predisposition for men was somehow written upon him, even if his family hadn't been attentive or observant enough to notice it. Tacitly, Father had possibly understood or held suspicions.

But surely, he'd been under more duress before. He knew he had. Besides, had he not done away with one of the greatest sources of duress in his life and taken things into his own hands for once? It had been so simple to add a little more laudanum to Michael's tea that night, a whole dropperful to add to the other dropperful taken throughout the day—"What are you thinking about?" Lucas was at his back, and warm breath was on his neck.

"Nothing."

The breath turned into teeth, not too hard of a bite, but a bite all the same. "You feel like a thundercloud."

Surprised, Bertie said, liking the bite and confused that he was being questioned even gently, "It woke you up?"

"No," said Lucas, tempering his bite with a kiss, "a night-bird did that, or a very early bird."

Now that he mentioned it, there was a bird calling from somewhere near the window in the wall with all the cracks. "It's near dawn."

"How long have you been awake?"

"Hours, I think," said Bertie, "but I can't say for certain."

It seemed like centuries. He had woken with a gasp from a dream he could not recall, which probably meant it was not prophetic or at all important. This was discouraging, for he always remembered the ones that came to pass. Paired with the way none of the ones with Alastair had yet happened, he was doubting, increasingly, the veracity of what he'd glimpsed—happiness, bliss, the two of them passing time together in their own world. It unseated his sense of self, as well as his sense of purpose.

"Bertie, I do worry this obsession with our mutual friend will do you in."

"Perhaps it already has."

To that, Lucas pulled at his torso, clearly wanting him to roll over, and Bertie did, meeting his eyes in the relative dark-ness. There was little light, far more birdsong than light, and he could just make out Lucas's face and eyes. "Then...stop it," Lucas said.

"What do you mean?"

"Call it all off, whatever you're telling yourself you want to do. If you really wanted to do it, I think it would have happened by now. You're playing like a child, now—just let him go. This isn't the same as capturing crows and playing God."

"I should never have told you about that."

"I'm the only person you could tell who wouldn't refer you to a doctor or an institution."

"Perhaps that is so," said Bertie. "I never felt judged."

He thought about the first conversations they'd had on the subject, held in quiet tones at a corner table in The Sow. At the time, he might have been trying to impress Lucas, who even as a very young man had been party to violent things, the likes of which Bertie could not quite imagine even if he did have a brother who was insistent upon drugging him.

The circumstances of Lucas' world felt to him more like those out of a story, a fiction meant to entice and keep a reader invested in abstract experiences. In some small way, saying he could be party to something so grisly felt like it helped ensure Lucas' continued interest in him.

Their talks and time spent in Lucas' room, conversely, were not as much about impressing him—by then, Bertie did not think he might become bored. Those times were warmer, and no less vulnerable.

"I never judged you, but it did concern me. You were dabbling in things the likes of you shouldn't have." Softly, Lucas said again, "Let him go."

Lucas had always been perceptive. His choice of words, even now, when Bertie had communicated so little due to his need to control something, belied it. In truth, he wished he could call things off. He desired normalcy. But what kind would ever be open to him? He could not see his way to anything resembling others' lives, whether they were more like those of his parents, or Michael, or Lucas. Even Alastair and his blessed Mr. Apollyon.

He had been so sure as little as a week prior that he would have Alastair. That surety had eroded. He might have been weak in the first place to be so persuaded by seeing closeness, and the promise of as simple a joy as lingering in bed or elsewhere in his own home with someone who loved him. It was easy to despise himself for pinning so much on visions that were not even of anything monumental and extraordinary.

Although, one could say that for him, such reciprocal warmth was completely unexpected, so heady as to be intoxicating. Being wanted and treasured had a druglike effect upon him.

"I'm not sure I can."

"If I know anything, it's that most things can be walked back before a murder happens." Lucas grasped his hand, brought it to his lips, and kissed Bertie's palm. "Your skin is so soft." Then, he said, "There's been no murder. You could walk away from all this."

"Yes, there has," Bertie said, softly. Even if one did not count the crows, which he did, there had been a murder.

Lucas peered up at him, his eyes above his fingertips. "When?"

"Michael." Bertie had not thought he'd speak of it, and here he was, saying it so easily between the sheets.

He might have chuckled when Lucas's eyebrows knit together. "You said he was sick."

"Oh, he was."

"Did you *make* him sick?"

"No," said Bertie. "But I didn't let him recover."

Bertie had to admit the attempt had been halfhearted, more the sort of thing where he'd be content if it happened. If Michael lived, nothing about his own life would change.

He was not especially angry with how his lot had turned out, even if there were things he did not talk about. Had he been naught but a pauper, it was not as though he would shout in the street about having seen the next carriage accident before it happened, or of dreaming of another boy's very real suffering. But Michael had not woken up after all that excess laudanum, and so things had changed.

Seeming to need only a moment or two to contemplate this, Lucas nodded and kissed his palm again. "Clever of you. I never met your brother, but from your stories, I hated him."

That had been by design. Lucas was the first and only person he dared tell about Michael's abuses. Even then, he had not been truthful about how many times they'd occurred.

As a grown man, he could hardly admit to them without feeling somewhat ashamed, like he should have tried harder to make them stop. As a boy, he'd felt more strongly that he was weak to allow them to continue.

He had not planned on telling Lucas, it had just flowed from him one night at The Sow when they were fifteen or sixteen and Bertie was practicing his ability to sneak away. Mother and particularly Father were heavy sleepers, and the few servants who lived with them were too fond of Bertie to stop him if they'd even heard anything.

He would slip away and return before dawn, and once or twice, late enough to slink past Mrs. Yardley tending to her earliest duties.

But The Sow on that night felt safe, warm against a winter

night between school terms. Alcohol relaxed his tongue enough to tell part of the truth: his brother forced him to take small amounts of drugs in food or drink against his will, if only to see how he would react to them. He did not mention the darts, more in the rush of finally saying it aloud to someone, than out of omission.

Bertie recalled he'd nearly explained how he was almost sure he'd killed his first crow this way—intoxicated and without the means to know with surety. But he was too afraid that Lucas would scoff and might think him weak due to the admission of Michael's possible influence.

Lucas, though, did not scoff. He went very quiet and very still, then offered to *help*.

Bertie had said, "No, thank you," polite despite being a little stunned, and as time went on, he occasionally described more of the incidents Michael treated him to.

Each mention, Lucas would remind Bertie of his offer, to which Bertie would smile.

"I was ever so tired. I didn't truly think it through."

"What did you do?"

"Laudanum," said Bertie, "rather more of it than he needed."

He felt neither better nor worse having told Lucas, and really, there was no better person to tell. Lucas was hardly in any position to judge.

They had never discussed directly who Lucas had killed, or if he had killed, but it always seemed like a given thing. Bertie had been present when others—sometimes, others who eyed *him* like he was a mark, even though he took care not to dress finely when he ventured into Lucas' circles— casually mentioned acts of violence. Either Lucas had been present for it, as had been the case with one interrogation that had involved a beating, or he'd perpetrated it, as had happened with a robbery where he'd glassed someone.

He wondered if it might be useful to tell Lucas what else he was, besides a lazy murderer. Perhaps Lucas would not respond poorly to being told his new beau—if they were beaux now—was somewhat mad due to his visions. Whether he was being driven mad because of them, or because he largely hid them, he did not know.

Reality did not quite feel steady to him at present, and the moments it did now were often found in this bed with Lucas. He supposed it was healthier than killing birds, which even he could admit was a troubling thing to engage in. The knowledge might not have stopped him when he had been determined to feel the rush of a life snuffed out under his hands, but at least he could recognize it.

He had not known Will Lucas could quiet his mind and assuage his gnawing appetite. Something had drawn him to Lucas when they were children, and at the time, it was the drive for friendship and being good to someone else. Some of it was pity for a boy who was consigned to darkness when he was not shuffling about the city doing his dubious guardian's bidding.

He thought of the old bedroom he had seen, years ago now. As a matter of respect once they grew to know each other more, he tried not to attune himself to Lucas in such a way that would encourage visions about him. Of course, Bertie could not verify if the discipline was strictly helpful in that regard, but he supposed it was, for beyond that first association within his mind, there had been only a handful more. All minimal, at least from what Bertie saw or experienced.

A few were of Old Ross being violent. One was far more carnal: Lucas with a young woman their age in bed. That, Bertie had decidedly tried to shut out as best he could, because he didn't want to experience such a thing from Lucas' point of view. It seemed invasive, and it brought envy.

Another was similar to the vision featuring the woman, but with a man. That had elicited even more envy, but at least it blessed Bertie with the knowledge that Lucas might seek out men.

The thought of anything he'd seen being a fantasy was quickly dissolved when Lucas himself had corroborated many of Old Ross's abuses with an air of shame. Bertie, who was well used to shame, felt he'd had no reason to be ashamed of what Old Ross did to him.

He divulged nothing of what he'd seen in visions and merely provided a listening ear to an unlikely friend.

Now, he found he wanted to protect that friend, love that friend, and though the desire conflicted with what he had told himself he had wanted, it loomed in his heart. That, too, discouraged him, for what on earth was the point if he could not even have what he'd planned on? If he were to be truthful with himself, he knew his interest in Alastair had shifted from warm passion to avarice. It cut him as much as it sustained him, and some part of himself knew he should abandon it.

Unfortunately, he was familiar with what he should abandon and proficient in ignoring that familiarity.

IN SPITE of Bertie's agitation after telling Lucas what had happened to Michael, Lucas was pleased to discover he was amenable to kissing. Then more than kissing. He had fallen asleep not ten minutes after they had indulged in not-kissing.

Bertie's admission was not a shock, for Lucas had heard worse. He actually felt a faint air of satisfaction upon learning it. Michael had always been cruel to Bertie, and their parents had never reined him in, so far as he knew. It seemed they knew nothing of how insidious their older son was. They were clearly biased in his favor, and beyond that, tended to disregard Bertie's presence altogether.

Lucas could muster very little surprise at Bertie's actions.

One could only take so much before one snapped, and this was—as far as murder went—quite a tame instance. Still, Bertie had succeeded, no matter how incidental and tentative the attempt. He also benefitted from his social and familial status, for he was under no suspicion and most likely never would be.

From experience, Lucas knew such a success could make one more stubborn, even smug, or it might drive one to a brand of paranoia, or it might do both. Bertie seemed to be somewhere with both stubbornness and nerves. If he was successful in disposing of Mr. Apollyon now, even using Lucas's hand instead of his own, it might well shatter him. It was too much, too fast.

Killing should be acculturated to and carefully applied, even if one discovered a taste for it. Perhaps even especially if they discovered a taste for it.

After all, kill too many people in a row and the potential costs only grew. Being discovered might take time; it did depend on a number of factors. But the more anyone indulged, the more likely it was they would suffer a consequence, and those who were not absolutely sure of themselves tended to suffer most. He had to wonder if Bertie's success—as idle as it had been, apparently—in killing his brother, had unlocked this new fervor for Alastair.

If the fervor was more delusion and bloodlust than anything else.

Even Alastair had remarked he'd no idea how Bertie felt. Though there had always been an air of puppyish obsession on Bertie's part for him, it had come off more as comingled awe and sexual attraction. Not a man's passion.

He gazed at Bertie's sleeping face in the growing morning light, nervous to think this was love when it was so underpinned by protectiveness and affinity. He simply did not know love as well as matters of violence, but they seemed to coexist in his heart if he felt so protective over a fledgling murderer.

Because Bertie had seemed panicked in an unspoken way after his brief admission of poisoning his brother with laudanum, Lucas did the most obvious thing he thought he could do to distract him: seduce him. It had worked and Bertie had fallen back asleep, which was just as well, for he had nowhere to be and no responsibilities as such.

With a contented sigh, he thought if this was how life could be, he would not say no to more of it. *I was right when I said he was different.* The tedious walk back to Cromer had not been so long ago at all; he had told Alastair that Bertie felt more like them. At the time, he hadn't realized why. Now he knew.

As he studied a small crowd of freckles on Bertie's chest, he decided he would interfere before things seemed to escalate. It was not usual for him to care much what others got up to so long as they stayed out of his way—after all, the only reason he'd held a grudge against Alastair for so long was due to the way he'd ruined a set of plans.

But now, he possessed a deeply uncomfortable knowledge that he *wanted* whatever was starting to take shape between him and Bertie. Enough, perhaps, to make anything Bertie had planned go awry for his own good.

## 12

A calm, cold evening with clouds threatened a storm, but Paul, ambling to Miss Garland's cottage, did not think he would be caught in any rain. He'd seen enough evenings like this one, and the sky always seemed more overdramatic than it intended to be and cleared well before the small hours. Having been awake later than many people while tending to The Queen Anne's mundanities throughout his life, he'd made a casual study of night-time weather to stave off boredom.

Anyway, he would be indoors should inclement weather occur, and very likely eating some of Miss Garland's superb cake. If she ever retired from her profession, and Paul wagered that one day she would, she could open up shop as a baker who specialized in cakes. In return for helping her rearrange some of the furniture in her small home, she'd promised to feed him. He presumed she meant some kind of meal, but he just angled for sweets.

Amidst thoughts of what sort of cake, the call of his name interrupted him. "Mr. Apollyon?"

He could not place the voice, but turned to it all the same. Enough people were thronging about that it could be anybody; the light was fading but it was still trading hours for many businesses. A blond man who stood a couple of inches taller than him, dressed in clothing that likely cost at least a quarter of his yearly income, met his eyes.

"Yes?"

"I wondered if you might take a drink with me."

Something of a very odd request from a stranger while one was just going about his business and nobody had been introduced.

A sense of unease prickled; Paul had not shed his vigilance over any of the matters at hand, especially not if he was outside his own domain, such as it was. He allowed himself a moment to see if anything preternaturally strange emitted from the man, hoping he did not appear like he was staring. A drop in his stomach came when he considered this could be, had to be, Bertie. He was not unused to strangers who dressed well, but this one was uncommonly well dressed.

Paul could not summon enough belief for coincidence to feel right.

He caught nothing hugely out of the common way as he looked at the man's aura. The colors around him looked bruised, almost like old and mishandled fruit, a mélange of browns and purples. There might be any reason for them, and they were gone as soon as Paul blinked them away. He had to focus to see them, and sustaining it could be too much of a strain to do it at every turn.

Perhaps the stranger was ill in some way, or had experienced a bad day. Both things could change the swirl of personal colors around a person.

"My apologies," said Paul, "I'm actually on my way to a friend." Reflexively, he straightened his hat.

Although this fellow did not seem visually amiss in the normal way, some invisible quality of his made Paul want to put more distance between them. Almost like he sat too near a fire and it warmed him overmuch. While he wouldn't call it terrible, it was uncomfortable. By way of defusing some discomfort, he studied the man's face. They were likely not the same age, with the stranger having a few years on him, if not more. It was hard to tell with somebody in fine clothes, for they were generally favored by an easier upbringing that took less of a toll on the body.

Meanwhile, around both of them, the evening's trade carried on as normal, with people eddying near certain shops and stalls.

"I don't mean to be rude in presuming, but you and I are overdue in our introductions."

"Bertie." He did not feel inclined to be overly polite, or polite at all, but he did correct himself for the sake of it. There was nothing that would stop Paul from referring to him by the diminutive in his own mind. "I mean to say, Mr. Calder."

"Yes." Bertie appeared to be taking stock of him, now. He was genteel about it, but he was nonetheless peering at him, no doubt trying to determine what about Paul had attracted Alastair enough to keep his interest. Had he not wondered the same about Bertie? "You are really quite underwhelming up close."

It wasn't a true insult; it merely was something a bitter person would say. However, he still and always would resent that Bertie had watched him—from who knew how near—

with only the protection of old walls and pitted glass between them.

He thought about what Torquil had said, that Bertie sounded like Paul when he spoke, sometimes, and contented himself with knowing that Bertie probably hated the round, almost drawling syllables that cropped up for him about every fourth word. It was subtle, but he hadn't lost them entirely.

Doubtless, he concentrated harder around those who mattered more than Paul. There must have been some difficulty in maintaining the illusion of more proper speech when one was surrounded by the very way of speaking one wished to shed.

"If you'll forgive me, I would rather not socialize with a man set upon insulting me," said Paul, about to take a step away from Bertie and back in the direction he had intended to travel. "But you do know my place of work and residence, so if you should like to see me, I'm nearly always there."

"I do think we should talk."

"No doubt you do." Wary of the intensity in the short sentence, Paul continued to edge back from Bertie until he was stopped by a firm pair of hands at his back, the palms flat against his coat. Less confused than incensed, he glanced over his shoulder to meet none other than Lucas's eyes and could not muster the smallest amount of alarm when he cast aside some of his irritation. "So you liked Cromer enough to stay, I see."

"It has its charms."

It was not as though they could murder him in the middle of a populated street, even if dusk was falling, or so Paul told himself. Regardless of whether it would hold true, he drew himself to his fullest height and stood straight, asking Lucas, whose face was composed, "What's it to be, then? A gun at my back? Then a walk to the nearest body of water?" He could not resist a grim quip in reference to his vision, though it might register as nonsense to his companions.

So as not to draw anybody else into prospective danger, he kept his voice down. He would feel worse if someone tried to intervene and was hurt on his behalf.

He did not believe he imagined the confusion on Bertie's face, confusion that looked more like confirmation, but he was in no position to address it properly given his circumstances. Instead, he wondered if Alastair had actually been attracted to Bertie—who was not an ugly man, but in Paul's opinion lacked verve—or he had merely settled out of lust and loneliness. The latter seemed more likely.

The hard barrel of a revolver against his spine was his answer, but to any onlookers or passersby, it would be veiled by their coats. He was certain. With a sigh, he continued to keep his posture as perfect as it could be, not wanting to give either of these men the satisfaction of showing his nerves.

What startled him more than a gun, though, was Bertie grasping his wrist and turning it so that the soft underside of his arm was slightly exposed. Before he had a moment to protest or question what Bertie was doing, the flesh stung as though he'd scraped it against something or cut himself. Aghast at the sensation, he glanced down to see a small, feathered dart held carefully between Bertie's fingers.

It was nowhere big enough to be considered a needle, and he pocketed it carefully, almost as soon as he had used it. Feeling no ill effects yet, Paul met Bertie's eyes again. There must have been an unspoken question in his own. Bertie said, "I haven't killed you. Don't worry."

Lucas must not have been privy to this element of the plan, if there was much of a plan, for he said in a low and audibly confused voice, "What have you done?"

Paul could not decide if that confusion made him feel worse, or better. Worse, if it meant Bertie was unpredictable enough to go around scraping people with drug-dipped sharp objects. Better, if it meant Lucas might possibly help him. In truth, he did not want to ask Lucas for any help, and a small part of him understood being proud might contribute to injury or death.

"Nothing that hasn't been done to me."

Paul was still looking at Bertie and trying to understand what had just happened. He could spare little empathy for Bertie's phrasing.

Worry and consternation wove through Lucas's tone. "How the hell do you intend to talk to him if he's drugged, then?"

*Oh, Lucas, I don't think the intention was to talk.*

As though echoing Paul's thought, Bertie said, "I shall get him to the cab. You can take your leave—just a bit of privacy for us, please. We shall be at home."

And the intention wasn't even to have Lucas kill him. Were the present circumstances not terrifying, Paul would find them fascinating. Never had he met anyone for the first time who wished only to harm him.

**13**

———

After Bertie had summarily dismissed him, Lucas went directly to The Queen Anne, where he wagered or very much hoped Alastair would be. There had been no suggestion to him of any plan involving Michael's old tricks. There was only a general agreement that, if they ever happened to spy Mr. Apollyon out on his own, they would chivvy him into the cab and away in the name of intimidating him to give up Alastair.

Lucas did not quite believe he would, but Bertie still seemed to. Luck alone meant that on this steely evening, they *did* see Mr. Apollyon walking alone, wearing quite a cheerful expression.

In hindsight, he should have assumed Bertie might move forward with something on his own—and why would he not borrow from his brother's ominous strategies. A little dart, if it could be called such when it was not shot out of something, was small enough to conceal and could be kept in a wee glass vial or a bit of oilcloth to prevent whatever was on it from leeching out.

He might have intervened on the street, but for Bertie's eyes.

They had gone rather harried, and Lucas knew better than to cross any man who had the look of a cornered dog about to bite. He'd gotten the scar on his face when he'd tried to break up a street fight between a recently bereaved widower and his friend. Things started because the friend inadvertently insulted the dead woman, making a quip about her fidelity that was supposed to be a joke.

The wound had come from the widower, who'd possessed the same look Bertie did. A shard of glass in his hand did it quickly enough. Mistakenly, Lucas thought the widower would be easier to subdue because he was drunk and heartbroken. As his blood dripped to the floor, Lucas learned to treat such an expression with caution. Though he did manage to knock the man out, it was only done through searing pain and with much mess.

Emotionality could be an accelerant, not a hinderance.

He certainly reminded himself of it now, years later. Encouraged by the way Mr. Apollyon had not immediately lost consciousness, sagged to the ground, or gone pale, Lucas had left them both and headed for the public house.

Relief flowed into his mind when Alastair was where Lucas expected him to be, tidying up the taproom that looked like so many others but seemed to contain more abnormality than its peers.

He did not announce himself; Alastair faced the door leading to the entryway and spied him as soon as he entered the otherwise empty room.

"I thought I told you to leave. If I had known I had to take the journey with you to make you say put, I would have gone too." Understandably, Alastair was not pleased to see him and disapproval rang in his voice.

Were he in Alastair's position, he wouldn't be happy to see him, either. "Hello to you, as well." Rather than show he was disconcerted in any way, Lucas ambled right up to him and said, "I couldn't leave well enough alone." It was old conditioning to bluster and obscure how he actually felt around Alastair, or anyone, and even though he carried an extreme agitation over what Bertie might do, he could not break an old habit.

However, his nerves must have shown in his expression, for Alastair stopped wiping one of the tables in the taproom and said, "Have you got something to say?"

Tonguing the edge of his mouth, Lucas did not know where to begin. He had much to say and did not know if most of it was relevant. Bertie had not told him what he'd intended to do with Mr. Apollyon; Lucas had been made aware only that he was needed to get him into a cab. The easiest way to do that, when it came to most marks or targets, was a gun at the back, easily concealed by clothing or sleeves and even easier to hide in autumn or winter than when it was warmer outside.

That Alastair was not lunging for him, or even terribly surprised, was not in itself unexpected at all. They had come of age in a world where few actions matched words, or at the very least, most men were out for themselves in some way. There was little incentive to tell the absolute truth even to a friend or a colleague, and many of their ilk did not as a matter of habit.

It was an open secret that Lucas had pined for such a life that would permit him to live with less guile and more comfort and honesty. Of course, nobody addressed it, as that would be considered both rude and pointless. Very few of them managed to get away from their criminal leanings, and those who did were often regarded with an envy that masqueraded as derision. He didn't like, instinctively, that survival often required finessing the truth. He'd learned the art well under Old Ross's roof—as a matter of self-preservation, he rarely thought about the relentless abuse once he was out on his own.

Bertie, actually, had heard more about it than anybody, and it had been given largely after Lucas understood how dire the relationship between the Calder brothers was.

*Wrong,* Michael had apparently said to Bertie, *you're all wrong.*

At least Old Ross hadn't ever said something of the kind. Not about him being wrong. Indolent and spiteful, but not wrong just for the sake of wrongness.

He shook his head and tried to clear it of the past, for the present was of more immediate concern. He didn't fully understand why he had come here, but part of his reasoning was that Alastair had not actually killed him on the way to Trunch or under the ground once there—yet Lucas had read in his eyes how much he'd wanted to. He did not know if Alastair wished to appear more upstanding in front of his husband, or if he was embracing a new way of things, but the fact remained. Alastair had not killed him.

More importantly, too, was that Lucas did not believe Bertie would be able to come to terms with having killed Paul Apollyon, even if he succeeded. He might not be jailed; he might not go to the courts at all. It felt more likely that somebody might try to blackmail him for preferring men and being wealthy, therefore being an excellent target for such a maneuver, than he would ever face a trial or a judge for murdering an unknown public house owner from Cromer.

There were cracks in Bertie that Lucas could not begin to fathom, a spiderweb of little fractures that had come through a lifetime of slights and underestimation and his brother's abuses. Perhaps he was different from Lucas, who had certainly experienced his fair share of difficulties. One of them was fine china and prone to shattering, while the other had become tempered metal.

He could not help but wonder if it were more to do with Bertie's abilities. Not because he was superstitious, either, but because seeing the future—however wrong the sights might be, or even if they proved correct—seemed too much of a burden for any one person to bear. Lucas couldn't characterize it as a gift, and though he might not have believed it coming from another person, in this instance, he could not see why Bertie would lie.

Unless he truly was mad, in which case it was a delusion. But even the day they'd met, Lucas was aghast at how he had even briefly described that sour-smelling old room with the quilt. How could Bertie have lied or made that up? He was always ready to think everybody lied, and Bertie *had* lied about smugglers' gold, but in the matter of Lucas's bruised face and blue quilt, he'd told only the truth.

Lucas never told him what exactly had happened that day, the very afternoon after making the first delivery to the Calders' house and returning later than he should have to Old Ross. He had been too ashamed, and he hadn't wanted to upset someone who might be a new friend, even if that new friend had somehow been able to see his threadbare room.

*A boxroom,* Bertie had called it, years ago.

He'd been right. There hadn't been any windows in it, and before he'd arrived, it was used to store things. After he'd arrived, it was still used to store some things and the main concession to his presence had been a cheap bed. Lucas had always thought it bizarre that Old Ross kept him with the barest of necessities, making sure Lucas knew what a sufferance it was to have a child underfoot, but still insisted he learn to read—which he did quite well—write, and do some sums.

As silly as it was, he had hoped Bertie would be a friend, as vastly different as they were, and even at that young age, he'd been too aware of how awful the details of his life with Old Ross were. No worse than many others' lives when they were in his position, but just as bad.

"You look like you're watching a ghost."

He blinked and cast his eyes to the floor, then back to Alastair's face. "You didn't kill me that night, and you could have."

"You'll have to refresh my memory. There have been a few nights when I didn't kill you and could have."

"This most recent one, when we didn't find any fucking gold." Alastair played with him, and he'd had little appreciation for it. He rarely did under the best of circumstances. "But take them all into consideration, if you wish. I've come to tell you something, and I pray I'm wrong."

Finally, Alastair stilled and regarded him with an air of seriousness. Lucas had never been attracted to him romantically or physically, but even he had to admit that married life suited him well. He would never say so, as that wouldn't fit the tenor of their relationship at all, but he had lost the rather haunted look he'd had when Lucas first met him. It had only become more deeply embedded the longer they had associated, and having spent more time with Bertie privately, he knew it was somewhat to do with the weight of *shoulds* that had accumulated in Alastair's life.

He should get married. Truly married, to a woman. Failing marriage, he should find a woman to cohabitate with. A large of expanse of upright society still considered that immoral, but most people in the demimonde did not, or did not have a strong opinion on it. Everybody was too busy trying to survive to have deep thoughts on morality.

He should have a family. He should do the right things, including step away from a life of crime. Even that should weighed heavy, and Lucas knew it himself. Less the weight of who to marry than the continued burden of struggling to survive within the only means they had—firstly, Lucas thought he would be dead well before now, and marriage wouldn't be a question he considered, and secondly, his tastes encompassed anybody, women included.

But now that Alastair had embraced life in a way he never had, the results showed in his face, less drawn and haggard. His body, less taught with vigilance.

Lucas fought down a chuckle. At the precise moment, Alastair was more vigilant, but Lucas could not blame him. "Where's your Mr. Apollyon?"

"Out," said Alastair, and somehow the word was said slowly, though it was so short.

"Where?"

"He went to help a friend move some of her furniture."

"In the evening?"

"He didn't wait until closing." Alastair snorted and folded

the rag he had been using to clean. "I told him to go and stayed here to mind the place. I imagine they're just talking now. It's good for him to get out of The Queen Anne, sometimes. He so rarely does. And as you can see, it isn't busy."

Perhaps happiness had dulled Alastair a little too much.

The Alastair that Lucas knew would never have relaxed if Bertie were so near, and though Alastair still took his presence into account, it didn't seem he took it so seriously.

To be fair, the Bertie they had known had either kept a variety of urges to himself or finally developed them once he was free of his entire family. Again, Lucas was forced to wonder if being different, not only in who he loved but also in what he could do, had proven to be too much stress upon his mind in conjunction with years of neglect and maltreatment.

The way he had spoken of the crows had slightly unnerved even Lucas, who prided himself on his learned tolerance for hearing about cruelty and partaking in it. In his view, there was no other way to be within a world that seemed hellbent upon inflicting it. He might not always engage in it himself, and indeed, he had an amount of restraint compared to other men he knew. But the world itself did not generally echo such control.

More to the point, he did not like cruelty much—control was enough to make a point, and brutality felt gratuitous, especially when directed at anyone or anything who was essentially powerless to start with.

"I don't think he's with a friend."

Alastair's expression almost bored into him. "Where do you think he is?"

"With Bertie."

The muscles in Alastair's jaw contracted. "What the hell have you done?"

"It isn't what I've done, so much as what I've gotten myself mired in," said Lucas, and he toyed with telling Alastair about Bertie's ability, but that did not feel like his truth to tell. He knew it would be relevant to how Bertie had been behaving, or at least he speculated this was the case. Yet Alastair did not need to know in order for them to intercept Bertie and Mr. Apollyon.

"I told you he was mad for you..." here, Lucas swallowed, not positive if Bertie was, now. He suspected his erratic behavior might be for its own sake more than thoughts of love or lust. "But he's just...mad."

He did not think, whatever Bertie was up to, he would be adept enough to kill quickly. More to the point, he had the sense that Bertie would want to play with his food before he ate it, and they would have time to prevent the eating part. Of course, he might be wrong, but he felt he'd done his duty in coming to Alastair. Rescuing Mr. Apollyon was somewhat secondary to having spoken up, something he did not often do unless it absolutely concerned him.

A young maid, the same dark-haired woman who had brought toast the morning he had discussed Trunch and potential lost treasure, padded quietly through the taproom as though neither Alastair nor Lucas was there at all.

With a growled syllable that might have been a profanity, and knowing Alastair, was, he came around the table and stepped directly in front of Lucas.

Calmly, Lucas moved his left foot, lest Alastair step on it.

"What the hell has *he* done?"

"I don't know, but if you'd like, we can find them and discover that for ourselves. He said they would be at home."

The look Alastair gave him was one of stark terror. Then he veiled it, as was expected. Very few advantages ever came from showing each other weaknesses, though he could read Alastair's the same way Alastair would likely read his. And Alastair would not necessarily know to assume Bertie was capable of more extreme measures, the way Lucas now did.

But he knew about the crows. He could make the mental leaps.

"You had best hope," said Alastair, and he sounded louder and more like his old self than he had around Lucas these last several encounters, "he's safe. Or there will be hell to pay for you. I'm sure I can't kill Bertie without attracting attention I don't want, but you—"

"You wouldn't hang for your Mr. Apollyon?" Lucas couldn't resist needling him. He knew the answer was, Alastair would.

"Gladly. But if he was already dead, I'd far rather kill the man who did it and then turn my hand on myself. Why draw it out?" This was sealed with a wolfish grin. "If I was arrested, the torture would be in waiting to die and join him. But I would happily kill you, then myself."

"Better to hang for him if he lived?" Lucas asked, despising how romantic he thought all of this was.

"Just so."

"He would hate that."

A small spasm of sorrow passed through Alastair's mien. "I know he would."

Something quite uncharacteristic came from Lucas'

mouth before he could stop it. "Then we should find him before Bertie does something rash."

14

O ne of the most frightening things about being chivvied about while sedated in the place where he had lived his entire life was that nobody knew anything was out of the ordinary. He reckoned that their familiarity with him only strengthened perceptions nothing was wrong.

Paul Apollyon was certainly not known for his drunkenness, quite the opposite in fact, but far be it from anyone to intercept him while he was intoxicated with what seemed to be a gentleman of means.

If the younger Apollyon had taken it into his head to have a little fun for once, nobody wanted to interrupt it. He was such a quiet, serious fellow that some worried he might devote too much of his life to what he *had* to do and not enough to what he *wanted* to do. That was always the way of it, with serious young men.

So if he were ambling about with a fancy man in the late evening, who was anyone but his rumored beau to stop him?

This assumption was, of course, very likely part of Bertie's plan and it worked well.

It was not that so many people milled around, and more that those who did were proficient in minding their own business rather than interfering with others' affairs. The distance to the cab, which Paul assumed was Bertie's own private one, was also not long enough to attract much attention. Other details escaped him; he did not know who drove the cab, he did not know where they were going, and he did not know precisely how long it took to get there.

By the time they reached what Paul hazily assumed was Bertie's family home in Cromer, or just near to it, all Bertie needed to do was steer him to a large, still pond ominously lit by the few stars peeking through mulish clouds. They did not stop directly at the pond; instead Bertie kept marching him to a small outbuilding that had seen better days.

Paul still had no impetus to flee. Whatever Bertie had pricked him with, his body found it seductive. He was warm, and his limbs seemed weighted. Though his tongue was in his mouth, he might swear it lolled. Now, he wasn't even particularly worried, even if the knowledge that he was being pushed toward something menacing and no one seemed to know it should trouble him. Any sense of fear felt truncated, like something he might revisit in a nightmare or later by a warm fire.

Even the rejoining thought that there might not be a later felt hard to reach.

"What did you do to me?"

"My brother used this on me a fair few times," said Bertie. Paul noted, not for the first time, that Bertie had decidedly let his natural accent slip through.

Though his limbs appeared to need a little more direction from an outside force, his voice was less impacted. "What is it?"

"I can't give up all my secrets, but Michael assured me it was safe. I suppose it is, after all, because I'm still here. I can tell you, though, that he had access to all sorts of mad things while he was at Cambridge studying the sciences and medicine. If it wasn't from there, he snuck it from Father's cupboards." Bertie nudged him inside the outbuilding, which was empty save for various gardening implements and a frail wicker chair. "I found some of the stuff left in his bedroom, in a little vial. I knew it by smell. Somehow, it always put me in a nearly cheerful mood—or, at least, a biddable one—even if my higher reasoning objected to whatever macabre thing Michael was doing."

Paul had no real knowledge of sedatives or hypnotic compounds, but he had read enough gothic novels to know they could be used to great and nefarious effect. This one didn't stop him from sneezing, though, when the dust of years of minimal use met his nose. "Cheerful is a stretch. I feel like a puppet."

His words were not slurred. Before he had ventured to speak moments ago, he had not been sure if they would run together, as a drunk person's might.

"You are being a most agreeable puppet." Bertie seemed serene now that Paul was drugged; it would have been a startling change had he not been under the influence. "Sit on the chair."

Without thinking of what might come next, Paul sat, gazing up at him and wondering how Bertie and Alastair had looked together in bed. It was a vulgar topic, perhaps, but he could not help the stray thought. If one went for his type, Bertie was handsome in a louche way. The loucheness wasn't just present because of how he behaved. It lurked in his demeanor, like cheerfulness or warmth might for another person. His actions were only making the disrepute more apparent.

"When did you fall in love with him?"

"Pardon?" Bertie had his back slightly turned to Paul and he was reaching for something on a little shelf. "Oh, I see. You mean Alastair."

As Bertie turned back around, Paul could not summon nearly enough alarm at the rope in his hands. "You know, you could just *tell* me to get in the pond."

"I have heard drowning is an awful way to die, and that those who are rescued say they did everything they could to survive it."

So he was to be tied to a chair to prevent his body from making attempts at living. "Did you make a study of it?" If so, he might not be amazed. All of what Bertie knew seemed rather unpleasant.

"Not specifically of drowning, but death? Yes." Scratchy, hardy rope wound around Paul's wrists as Bertie drew them both back to secure them. In a way, his frightening vision had been correct, or it had tried to be. He had sunk through water, ankles and wrists bound, no chair, and there had been two voices in the lead up to it. The realities were different and no less dire. He was still tied up, and one man could evidently do what two might have accomplished. "From time to time, I have found myself interested in it. My father was a physician, and I suppose some of that had to surface in my blood."

Unbidden, Paul wanted to ask if Bertie had made a study

of death more because he wanted to die himself. Instead of venturing to ask that, he said, "Your brother."

"What about him?"

Silk scarves and ropes crafted for bedroom play felt much better than this did, and Alastair was much faster at tying him up than Bertie was. The same as the subject of suicide, he did not think the topic of sex would be a welcome one in this conversation. Especially if it pertained to sex with the man Bertie wanted to have for himself.

"Did he really die of an illness?" Bertie had not told Paul that himself, so Paul added, "Lucas mentioned it on our walk back from our fool's errand."

A soft laugh came from behind him, then, and Bertie replied after a moment's pause. "There is no harm in telling you the truth."

"Not if you are about to drown me in your pond." It was agonizingly obvious what Bertie was going to do and were Paul in his right mind, he would be doing everything in his power to stop it. He would be thinking of Alastair, of Edward, of Miss Garland and Benson, of the silly but exquisite little life he had.

Instead, he was asking a murderer of crows if he had also murdered his brother.

"Michael *was* ill. I believe he would have died had I waited, but something tipped my hand." By the time Bertie finished his last sentence, Paul's torso was fully bound to the chair. "I should be thankful it was so simple. He had no wife. There was no heir." Wistfulness was in his tone, if Paul had his measure.

Sighing, Paul said, "So you didn't *want* to kill him."

His answer sounded tired and frank. "It was not premeditated. I had no plan, and the idea did not occur to me until... well, it was rather late in the evening, and...I simply did it. Gave him more laudanum than anyone could withstand, really."

These were not the words of a wanton murderer, and yet, here Bertie was indeed trying to murder him.

That Bertie was unwell was obvious, and had not Paul said he seemed so? The why of it was less obvious, but in Paul's compromised and drugged physical state, Bertie's sickly purples and muddy browns and putrid yellows were easier to catch even in semidarkness. Something more begged for Paul's attention, but he was not able to define it as it lurked in the shadows of his mind. Something about Bertie felt rancid to him, and the unreal colors around his body were as oddly distorted as they were bruised.

If one turned from oneself so cruelly, Paul could only imagine the consequences. If all one had heard about oneself was to be seen and not heard, or if no tenderness had ever been extended to them, he could only guess at the repercussions into adulthood.

Was it only these things, or was there something more?

Any kind of satisfaction at being proven right about Bertie's instability was as difficult to reach as curiosity about the subject. In truth, neither would help him.

As Paul tried, minutely, to move his arms and hands, Bertie moved on and bound his ankles to the chair's legs. He hoped, although it was a faint, ambiguous sense of optimism, Alastair would appear and prevent him from being dragged to a pond and discarded. Funny, since having that terrible vision of sinking through dark water, he had not once thought it might be a pond.

It also had not come to pass that anyone with an accent like Alastair's was speaking, which was notable, but what stood out to Paul most was the dull nature of the body of water. The broads, the rivers, the sea, all of these felt mightier than a pond.

In addition to fixating upon this mundane little detail, he recalled in brief the vision of Lucas saying, "You have to stop him, you see?" and felt, if he did get out of this, he would make a study of any premonitions that presented more like allegories, or strange spiderwebs of realities.

He could not begin to think how he could have stopped anybody.

Perhaps a circumstance had changed between now and then, however short the time was that had passed, and his connections to whatever provided the premonitions were trying to acclimate and warn him. He feared under the soft, drugged haze that it would not matter at all.

"Where the fuck do you think they've gone?" When he and Lucas approached the open gate to Bertie's house and faced the empty expanse of lawn with the house directly ahead at the end of a graveled drive and an enormous, ornamental duckpond to their left, Alastair tried to command his heartbeat to slow. It wouldn't, not until he had Paul in his sight, but he made the attempt to calm himself all the same. "It's a big fucking house."

Nothing good would come of him losing his head.

Lucas's mouth gaped open a little as he appeared to think, not that Alastair wanted to be privy to his thoughts save for this one, and then his eyes settled on the grass before them.

Alastair followed his look and eyed the pattern of disturbed blades, hard to make out at night, but distinct enough if one had any experience tracking somebody else. The cold air helped him to think more than a mild night would have. He did not see footprints, or nothing distinct enough to mark a trail of two sets of them, but there was a suggestive trail from the edge of the lawn to the duckpond.

Without hesitation, he said, "The pond." All the trepidation over that damned vision, and he had only ever thought about the sea or, when he was feeling especially macabre—because he did not like the idea of Paul's body being swept inland rather than up onto a beach—a river or the broads.

He took off at a clip, caring little if Lucas kept up with him or not. The lawn was far too large for him to be comfortable strolling, even if he might have admitted under calmer circumstances that the element of surprise could be of importance now. Bertie might have a gun or a weapon, but an unspoken whisper told Alastair his means of persuasion would be softer yet no less deadly. His instincts and observations were rewarded when, as he squinted toward the outbuilding, an unwieldy silhouette moved against some trees' distinct outline.

Lucas panted at his side as they ran. "There they are."

Alastair kept all his focus on moving. The silhouette, which proved to be Bertie dragging a chair with Paul atop it, was making its halting way to the pond. The sheer inefficiency of having chosen to, he presumed, bind Paul to a chair, might just grant them enough time to intercede. The space between them, and Bertie and Paul, was agonizing, the sort of thing Alastair had only experienced in a nightmare.

It was closing, but not nearly fast enough, and even though Bertie was not particularly strong, Paul was a slight man.

Once he was near enough to shout and be understood, he barked, "Give it up, Bertie."

Lucas's mumbled words of caution were not enough, and they were too late.

Bertie looked in their direction, and Alastair would have sworn he smiled when he tipped the chair into the water.

---

THE VERY LAST thing he heard before he went under was Alastair's voice, which suited him. It might be the final human thing he heard, so he tried to hold fast to it against the rush of water in his ears. An effect of whatever substance he'd been given was the continued calmness, unnatural and unhelpful as it was, and this allowed Paul to reflect yet again upon how the present moment and his premonition were different.

In the vision, he'd been bound at the wrists and ankles, but not to a chair, and there had been two voices speaking near him. Bertie was acting alone with not even Lucas to help him, his actions seemed impulsive and possibly not communicated to his—

*Lover, or hired help?*

The cold was indubitably the same between the two visions. He had always disliked being cold, but whether from fear or physical effects, it was the coldest he had ever been.

Under the artificial calm, he knew he was panicked; it was there like the sediment at the bottom of the pond, unseen and also an inevitability.

Perhaps his abilities had tried to warn him as best they could, but his own visceral fear had muddled them as the experience came to pass, or perhaps this was like one of the far more mundane things that had proven different from what he'd first seen. He did not know how time worked, and far more intelligent men than him no doubt had trouble with the concept even without the preternatural.

A philosophical or metaphysical question for another day, if he survived.

He could hold his breath well enough, and if he hadn't been stuck to a chair, he could swim quite well too, but soon neither skill would matter. His eyes were open, but he could see nothing given the night's darkness. Weeds clung to him, and bubbles flurried around him, tickling his nose.

It was a deep enough pond to kill a man, and having been raised near the sea and the broads as well as rivers, he knew there did not need to be much water for someone to drown. He wondered if, at this point, Bertie even cared whether Alastair would be with him after he'd done something like this. It might not matter to him now, or if it did, he was so far from any rationality that he had not considered how murdering Paul would impact Alastair's benevolence.

Once the chair settled at an angle against something solid and slightly soft, Paul's lungs had started to burn, and the sensation edged out some of his drugged tranquility. He had no sense of time other than one anchored by his lungs' vulnerability, and that time was running from his hands as they burned more even while his body grew colder. He was sure fear, as drugged as he was, made the water feel freezing. The cold had been so stark in his initial premonition.

As he started to consider the merits of taking as deep a breath he could just to hasten the inevitable, two ghostly hands appeared in the cold, pitch-dark water, visible merely due to their proximity and paleness.

LUCAS DID NOT BELIEVE in penance, but this might fit the definition. He would call it his one good deed, if good deeds could really be motivated by the thought that someone would kill you should their lover perish in a Norfolk pond. Alastair might not kill Bertie on sight, or at least Lucas hoped that was not happening as he groped for Paul Apollyon in the frigid, wet dark.

And surely he himself did not carry the same protection of sentiment and pity as Bertie did. He'd also pulled Alastair's tail too many times of late.

He supposed Bertie had, as well, but the fact remained that Alastair did not seem to pity Lucas nearly as much as he did Bertie.

His hands met with what felt like a human chest, and he prayed some other recently-in-residence Calder or errant groundskeeper had not used this pond in a similar way to Bertie.

The last thing he needed was to find a corpse and not Mr. Apollyon amongst the weeds. He ran his hands from chest to shoulders and was satisfied this was who he sought, not some unholy and awful body given any time to bloat and rot under the water.

His arms protested as he lugged the chair with its human attachment to the surface. Absentmindedly, it occurred to him that either luck or serendipity helped him locate Paul. He'd seen where he had gone in, and that had helped, but there was no visibility once under the water.

He had to say, he would never repeat something like this again. Hard enough to help someone with all the use of their limbs through any water if they'd been somehow incapacitated or they could not swim. This was next to impossible.

With a great gasp once he broke through the surface, it took all the strength he had to bring the chair with him when he haltingly found his feet and stood. Then he propelled both man and chair to muddy land. Mr. Apollyon would manage if he broke an arm; the most important thing was to get him to air, not ensure he was unscathed.

Alastair, predictably, went directly to wherever the chair had landed with its quiet and irrefutably solid thump.

Lucas was too occupied with catching his own breath and sorting through all the shame, guilt, and dismay permeating his heart. He was not sure if he would go so far as to say he was at fault for this—although if he were to be completely honest, he was in some ways—but he still wanted Bertie, which felt both pathetic and ill-advised.

Or, possibly it meant they fit with each other. He would not have thought little Bertie had the teeth for something of this nature, but he did. It might not have been teeth sharpened by necessity or lack, but they were sharp all the same.

*Wouldn't have thought he saw the future, either.*

Cold swept through him while he impartially looked on as Alastair, quick as a flash of lightning, cut the ropes keeping

Mr. Apollyon on the chair and eased him to the ground. Of course he still carried a knife.

In Lucas' professional opinion, he had to admit the chair was a neat bit of insurance against the panic brought about by drowning.

A quick glance told him Bertie already lay on the grass, likely having been knocked out cold by Alastair. Or killed. He did not truly think so, but he knelt near Bertie's prone form and brought two fingers to his chest, then his exposed neck. A pulse fluttered against them. Angry with Bertie yet again, this time for his rashness, if indeed it could be considered rashness and was not pure irrationality, he stepped from Bertie to Mr. Apollyon.

After a few moments, Mr. Apollyon took a great breath and started coughing, fit to retch.

"Welcome back," he said coolly, as he glanced from Bertie and back to Mr. Apollyon and Alastair.

It didn't garner a look, not even from Alastair, who might otherwise have objected to the tone. He seemed to be restraining himself from touching Mr. Apollyon until the latter stopped coughing, knowing it would do little good to help any of the heaving.

At last, the heaving quieted and, shivering, Mr. Apollyon dragged himself closer to Alastair. "Think I'd like to go home now. Have a bath. Never...go outside again." His speech was not slurred, but still held a halting quality beyond that granted by shivering, and the night was not freezing even if it was cold. Lucas conjectured that however Bertie had managed to abscond with Mr. Apollyon, it involved some manner of chemical that slowed reactions, the mind, and perhaps even the emotions.

Then he thought back to the elder Calder, Michael, and frowned, knowing his experience with tinctures, poisons, and chemicals.

An ache of empathy for Bertie, one he was not entirely familiar with, took root. He would not decide what to do with it here and now, but he did not think it would leave him.

It almost drowned out the resounding envy when Alastair said, soft and assuring as anything to Mr. Apollyon, "We can go home. I'll draw you a bath. We might have to go outside again, sometime, but I won't rush you."

He did not want Alastair, and he certainly did not want his landlord, but he wished for someone to speak to him that way, and to mean it without any divisions or hesitancies in their heart. As he returned his attention to Bertie, who looked almost serene with his eyes shut and on his back on the grass, he allowed for the possibility that if Bertie was not that person now, he might learn to be in the future.

It was more enticing than anything he'd ever told himself for comfort, and if the glimpses of the tenderness he'd seen within Bertie were anything true, it might become something.

*Might* was the most beguiling word he knew. Despite a lifetime of *mights* disappointing him, he was willing to place his faith in yet another. Perhaps he was madder than Bertie had ever been.

**15**

———

Paul had been asleep for an entire night, and the full day after, verging into another night, before Benson came home from Norwich with fewer things on his person—and the ostensibly immediate knowledge that something had happened while he was away. This happened to be due to little more than what Paul had said to him before he had gone, rather than a preternatural awareness that only he had.

"He *sent* you away?" Alastair asked, his plate largely untouched before him. Late evening found him and Benson eating in the kitchen, well after any customers had gone home and all external doors were locked for the night. Had the company been different, the atmosphere would have been romantic, the walls flickering with candlelight and embers in the hearth keeping things warm.

"I don't mean to say I think he knew what was going to happen," said Benson, after a hearty bite of his sandwich. Alastair's culinary skills were too basic to afford them anything more. "He might have had a sense. But I felt it was more that he fretted your former beau—"

"Bertie wasn't my beau."

"Paul fretted he would come here."

"He'd already been here."

"Can usually visit a place more than once," said Benson.

Rather than laugh at the dry tone with which the words were delivered, Alastair forced himself to take a bite of his own sandwich. Paul was all right, if exhausted, and he had been put to bed after a careful and adoring bath. Alastair had drawn the water himself, as nobody was available to help with the task, and it had been longer than any bath he'd provided or taken. But Paul was warmer and cleaner after the endeavor, and he fell asleep almost immediately after being clothed again in a soft, old shirt.

The bread was too dry, or his thoughts were too jumbled, for he coughed once and returned to his tea, which he had also abandoned while talking to Benson. He'd come to a Queen Anne that was in slight preternatural disarray. Thankfully not visible or physical disarray, for Alastair was proving competent enough at mimicking the landlord's duties at least for short periods. He found he quite liked working with people and serving the public.

Any preternatural undercurrents had to be awry, though, because upon entering the taproom, the first thing Benson had said to Alastair was not, "Where is Paul?"

It was, instead, "What happened to Paul, lad?" and all Alastair could do to keep from telling the story then and there was smile and shake his head. Neither of these Benson accepted, from the shrewd look given in reply, but he did not press Alastair further.

Rather than ask again, he had taken out his flask, settled in a corner, and drank until closing, at which time he did come to help tidy the place before bed.

Now they found themselves here with mediocre sandwiches filled with leftover roast chicken and tea brewed strong enough the wake the dead.

"I should have known," said Alastair quietly.

"What should you have known?"

"Paul was right to be more suspicious of Bertie, and I *saw* the look in his eyes. I should have been more vigilant against what he could do, and instead, I assumed he would be rather toothless when it came to anything darker than..." he stopped himself, then finished with, "meddling." Delusional, was what he had been, not toothless, and Alastair wanted to discover why.

He had wanted Alastair, ravenously, but that desire had turned fetid. Apparently, it had also expired, for even Bertie could not assume someone would want to remain with him after he'd murdered their lover.

If repression alone had broken Bertie's mind, it had done so thoroughly. But Alastair struggled to blame that on its own; so many others bore its burden with far more grace or just ability. They might not be pleasant, but they were not meddlers or would-be murderers. What drove Bertie seemed better hidden, as well as more deadly, than so common a thing as repressing oneself.

"The man did kill crows to send you as valentines." If anything, Benson was gentle in his remark. "I wouldn't call that toothless."

"No. I should have seen it as a warning sign. Well, of a different sort than what I had assumed." In another life, Alastair knew he would not have been so relaxed, regardless of who was posing a threat. Love had softened him. "Really, I should have made Paul leave that night I came back from our first little talk."

The underlying changes in Bertie had been evident then, and he had been unsettled. He had no name for them, and he still did not. Whatever had instigated them, it materialized for Alastair in Bertie's sycophantic tenaciousness, the possessiveness. He did wonder now if Bertie had clung to something that felt familiar, perhaps in a bid to calm himself or have something of old to hold onto, some feature from a life now changed.

"But he didn't want to go."

Alastair thought about how relieved he had been to hear Paul was staying. Perhaps he ought not to have indulged himself, but then, he hadn't wanted to overstep himself and deny Paul the choice, especially not after the airing of his own deepest-held secrets. James, Evie, the source of the income that had allowed him to travel here and spend his time in service to the most unpleasant fence he'd ever met. He'd felt, and might feel for a long time, that Paul had the right to behave exactly how he wanted even if Alastair asked him to do otherwise.

It was not quite an eye for an eye, or at the least, he did not view it as self-punishment. In its way, it was a form of equality, for he had behaved precisely as he wished in withholding various truths.

"No," said Alastair. He watched a shadow flicker on the wall before him, caught by the notion that visions of the future seemed like flickering shadows themselves, static under some conditions and wavering or changing in others.

He wondered what would qualify as a preternatural draft or breeze, the type of thing that would make a candle gutter.

"Well," said Benson, and he had finished his sandwich in large bites by now, "I wouldn't take it to heart. He doesn't want to be parted from you. That doesn't mean you caused anything to happen, not with your lies of omission, or your past. This fellow, this Mr. Calder, he has free will like the rest of us."

"His might be a little cracked."

"He has it, all the same. We've had, all of us, things happen—things that should render us useless, or cruel." Before Benson took another drink of his tea, he poured something from his flask into it. Alastair never asked what and he suspected the answer would change at any time upon the whim of its speaker. "I do hope this is the last cruel thing he does."

"I wonder if I should just find him now and end it." Even as he spoke, he wasn't inclined to do it, a response that disappointed the younger versions of him. "And then, as I say it, I think I should allow him another chance."

"Why?" Benson's one-worded question was not a challenge, and if Alastair considered what emotion, if any, was in it, he found mild approval.

"There is more under all of this than I know," said Alastair, as he met Benson's eyes, cloaked in shadow and shifting candlelight. "And I think that has driven him to it. I have a sense this will be the end of his interference." Lucas, too, was a factor he had not considered, an element within Bertie's actions that might be purer than it first appeared.

In truth, Alastair was less concerned with what Lucas represented in all of this, but there was no way to deny he had always been oddly, grudgingly protective of Bertie. Unless he missed his guess, something about that tendency had either strengthened or transmuted into something else that was more adult and lasting, going beyond a sense of duty or care for a man so clearly marked as different from the demimonde.

It was Lucas, he somehow sensed, who would provide a foil to Bertie's own unrest. Madder things had been true.

***

LUCAS HAD CONSIDERED SUMMONING A DOCTOR, a physician far kinder than Bertie's father was and his brother had never attempted to be, because Bertie had not spoken for more than a day. It was only when the day closed on the second night after he'd tried to kill Mr. Apollyon that he finally uttered a sentence. Before then, he had washed his face, dressed and undressed himself, and even eaten sparingly, he had just not said anything.

"I think I was mad. I might be, still."

Looking up from his book, for he did enjoy reading for pleasure when the opportunity was available to him, he closed it. They had retired to the same drawing room, or not-a-drawing room, yet again, the whole house at Bertie's disposal and this space still seeming preferable to him over all others. The very few servants who came to maintain the property did not appear to think this was odd.

Lucas did not say anything to the kind of, *Yes, I reckon you were mad.* The desire to agree was strong, but he did not wish to goad Bertie into any kind of ashamed or reticent silence. "How do you mean, and why?"

"It is difficult for me to articulate," said Bertie, and he sat a little straighter in his plush, maroon chair. "My whole life, I have always felt different."

"You were." In at least two key respects, Bertie was different from the vast majority of people, his precognitive abilities being one of those factors.

A fleeting smile passed across Bertie's lips and vanished. "Well, I mean to say, I felt different and worked exceedingly hard at hiding it. I think, and I have thought about it since..." he glanced away from Lucas and gazed at the happy fire in the hearth, which Lucas had started just as they'd sat down. Though Bertie had not been speaking, it was rather straightforward to divine what he wished for or wanted to do. Though, Lucas might also be willing to admit it was only rather straightforward because he had made a study of Bertie.

"Since the night at the pond," Bertie continued, and Lucas took in his deflated, listless voice. "I believe something about *constantly* keeping myself to myself might have led me to feeling so...hungry, and restless."

It was an interesting concept, and Lucas said, "I can't see how it would have been healthy to stifle yourself for years." He had seen men repress all manner of things that might pose a disadvantage or a weakness, from very young men who cried after they were bested and hurt in a fight, to men grown who wished only for their mothers as they died ill in a bed or bleeding in a dark close. They would never have voiced such things, had peril or pain or death not been upon them.

"Of course, I cannot know if it's everything. But the visions, they feel like pulls on a lure."

"I've never been fishing."

"I think you can still understand the metaphor," said Bertie, and his smile was now larger. "I could ignore most of them, when they happened, up until..." the smile shrank.

"Michael?" asked Lucas, and for him, the tone was kind. He meant, and did not want to say, up until Bertie had killed Michael. Had the crows been harbingers, or inoculations of a sort against full madness? He couldn't decide, for conventional wisdom said men who killed one thing were prone to looking for another, but it might have well been that a younger Bertie was driven to seek certain outlets by an excess of...

*Magic?* If these visions were such, anyway. His father had also been religious by reputation and rather strict in his beliefs. Bertie had also said so in brief. To be anything other than completely ordinary under such a man's roof must have been daunting, to say the least.

Yet an explanation could not be an excuse, or they were all lost. He did not quite feel that he wished to excuse himself for some of the things he had done, even though he could understand why he had done them. He sighed and shifted in his own armchair. Maybe excess laudanum in Michael's tea had been a step too far, and pushed Bertie into a place he had not been prepared to go.

Wherever that was, Bertie was no longer alone, for he had Lucas.

"Yes," Bertie said, "and then coming here...ever since I arrived, I have felt...different."

"How?"

"Disconnected, or maybe connected to something I am not used to."

This, Lucas knew, was in reference to things he would never experience, and they had to be realms of conjecture for all but the most well-versed person in things like spiritualism, or folklore. "Hell, Bertie, it might be something so simple as the weather or the ocean or eating all the crab." He tried to lighten the subject of discussion without trivializing the matter. "We'll get you somewhere else, London or Edinburgh, perhaps, and you shall be able to discover who you are with a person who knows what you can do."

"We?"

"Yes, indeed."

## 16

His awareness of the world came like an unexpected slap. Paul inhaled deeply but kept his eyes shut, less afraid than he was trying to adjust to being alive. It was not an unpleasant state, merely a slightly unexpected one, even if it became far more apparent to him as seconds passed that he ached too much to be dead. He wished to believe that if one did die, one hurt far less than this in the afterlife.

All the same, the pain was a happy reminder of surviving.

"Angel, you're safe." It was Alastair from somewhere near his left, quiet and calm. Paul wiggled both his legs, then his arms, satisfied he was no longer bound. He knew by scent he was in his room, their room, a hint of his own jasmine soap running under linens about a week out from washing. Vaguely, like he registered the shape of a building through fog, he remembered Alastair had helped him bathe, as tenderly and gently as one would any infant. He was glad of it, for he must have been filthy after his unwilling dunking in the pond.

Then he cleared his throat, partially to distract himself from the new pain that ebbed through his limbs, one that felt different from bruises and overexertion, and seemed to trace along the muscles themselves. Being tied up in such a fashion had aftereffects he had not considered. "I didn't drown." It felt likely they were both thinking of when he had dreamt of being cast into deep, cold water. He was, somewhat, and marveling that death hadn't claimed him.

"No." At that, Alastair reached for his chest and put a warm hand on his sternum. "Lucas fished you out."

"And you're sure Lucas helped?" He hadn't said anything to Alastair about his more recent vision containing Lucas' ambiguous words. *"You have to stop him, you see?"*

He had been too unnerved and preoccupied to bring it up. Beyond that, he'd been unsure of what it might signify. Retrospect might grant him more clarity, as it often did, and maybe one day soon he would elaborate upon it. In safety, before a cheery fire, and once all of this felt a little less nightmarish and more behind him.

"Aye, that he did," murmured Alastair.

Paul opened his eyes at last, and his suspicions that he was in his own bed were confirmed, not that any truly lingered. Alastair's shadowed eyes spoke of exhaustion, and he wondered how long he had been asleep or unconscious. The last moments he remembered before the warm bath were not at all comforting, and they tallied in some ways with his vision of sinking through dark depths—what he had thought was a prelude to drowning, even after waking and being held by Alastair.

To think it had all happened in a reasonably local pond. He pondered what use that initial premonition had been, but at least it had conveyed how cold he was to be. Some of it had to be fear mingled with the physical temperature. *And the effect of whatever Bertie slipped me.*

"I was drugged with something," he said, fighting against how dry his mouth was to form the words. "He had a needle, or a dart, I think." It was the faintest of recollections, like trying to recall a childhood nightmare that lingered only with sensations and suggestions of terror.

Moments of silence passed, and Alastair's fingers dragged on his skin. Paul had learned there was little point to rushing him, and whatever he would say would be said, but it was difficult not to let impatience creep through his usual desire to let Alastair come to him, or express himself without any coercive inducements. Perhaps he was wrong to be so permissive, but if he were to change his approach now, he would be trying to change himself.

It was not in his nature to push for things out of others, and he knew this had made him a relatively successful landlord in his own right. Still, he was rather shattered by Alastair's own permissiveness and the continued presence of someone like Lucas, who even if he was not as nefarious as Bertie, had clearly been an accessory to Bertie's goals.

"I *knew* there was something between them," he said, when Alastair did not speak. "And may I have some water, please?" He glanced at the small pewter pitcher on Alastair's nightstand with some longing, and Alastair obliged by pouring him a little glass and brought it carefully to his lips. Paul rather enjoyed being administered to in such a way, and it lessened the newly troubling sensation of water being inside his mouth again. Hopefully, it would fade.

"There wasn't," came Lucas's voice from the doorway that

led to the parlor and second bedroom, both of which were too close for Paul's comfort if Lucas was concerned in the equation of proximity, "until there was."

"He used you. I hope you see that." Paul believed that any relationship anybody had with Bertie would always be inequitable, and not just because it made little sense for a man of Bertie's social position never to take a wife. No man in Lucas's position could hope to gain his attentions or affections in a genuine fashion.

"No polite thank you?"

"Since I was under the water, I have no way of knowing what you did," said Paul, sitting up because he refused to be so vulnerable while Lucas was present. He was confused as to why Alastair was saying nothing, and winced with the headache that blared to the front of his senses as soon as he moved. "It would have been far better never to have been kidnapped, but I suppose a tiger can't change his stripes."

He wasn't positive if the tiger in question was Lucas, or Bertie. Perhaps it did not matter. Stepping further into the bedroom, Lucas exchanged a glance with Alastair, then shook his head as if in answer to Paul's question.

He looked remarkably like he had when Paul had first met him, when he had stepped into the taproom after closing and coolly declared Alastair *owed him*. In truth, his clothes had changed, perhaps because Bertie had furnished him with more in the days he had been here and keeping out of anyone at The Queen Anne's sight. But his demeanor and bearing were as calculated and vulpine as ever.

Despite wanting to tell him to leave, Paul did not. He needed to hear what Lucas said more than he needed to assert dominance over his own space.

"He didn't plan that with me," was not what Paul thought he would hear. "Abducting you. He didn't tell me what he planned on doing. I don't know what his plan was, or if he even had one."

"Pardon me?"

"If anyone was supposed to scare you, it was going to be me."

Still having uttered nothing, Alastair exhaled as though annoyed, yet was attempting not to give into too much of the annoyance.

Paul said, "Did you stay in Cromer because you knew he wanted you to be muscle?"

Taking his time to reply, Lucas glanced out the old window, the sunlight falling on the white strands in his hair before the curtain fell closed again. He had, as he seemed wont to do, forgone a hat indoors. "I stayed because I wanted him to give me answers."

"About that ridiculous farmhouse in Trunch?"

Lucas just nodded. It seemed Alastair was not the only reticent conversationalist with a criminal background.

"Did you ever find out if his relatives were real, at least?"

To that, Lucas shrugged. "They might have been. I think there were people who inspired the story...he said he had cousins who hanged. But like Bertie seems able to do, he persuaded me to stay and help—"

"Get rid of *Mr. Apollyon*." It was the first thing Alastair had said to Lucas, and the spark in the question was immensely attractive, as well as reassuring.

"I wasn't going to."

"Like hell you weren't."

But Paul, eyeing Lucas as he chewed his lower lip, wasn't

so sure. Lucas' demeanor did not speak of callousness right now, and Paul would never assume him capable of boundless kindness, but he supposed anyone could decide enough was enough. Regardless, logically, if not emotionally, it made sense to him that Alastair would want to keep Lucas close rather than force him out of the building.

He did not love seeing Lucas in his private flat, but he could appreciate Alastair's preferred manner of having him nearly within eyesight. Given the way they'd assumed he had left when that had not, in fact, been an accurate thing to believe, they probably should be able to watch him at the moment.

"I never wanted to."

"Why?" Paul asked, once a few moments had passed. "Why not?"

"I didn't want him to cross that line," Lucas said, half-turning so that he was just barely in profile to both the bed and Alastair, who sat beside it. "He was already courting madness, and I thought killing—even through me, by a technicality—might break him. Hell, he's already broken."

"You love him," said Paul. The nascent sense of jealousy he had caught from Lucas on that walk home was not here in his words now, but it allowed Paul to catch a deeper amount of feeling in how Lucas presently spoke.

Alastair tilted his head to look at Paul, then Lucas, but his expression was indecipherable as he did.

The answer from Lucas was not verbal, but Paul did not necessarily expect it to be. He merely smiled in the most ghostly, barest fashion, and a small amount of pink came into his cheeks. Unlike some of his red-haired peers, he was not heavily freckled; the color surfaced on pale skin like a bit of watercolor paint washed from a brush in clean water.

It was not lost upon Paul that a certain element of tragedy was in the situation, for Lucas was not Bertie's first choice and might never be even if they remained together. His thoughts returned to a wife who was not present yet, and all the trappings of the life Bertie was supposed to embody. Lucas would be secondary. He opened his mouth only to shut it again.

But Alastair's low, lovely voice sluiced through his burgeoning pity. "Take him back to Edinburgh."

Much to Paul's surprise, Lucas said, as though in immediate agreement, "He's in no state to keep a grand house here. The smaller one in New Town might well be better."

"Take him back," said Alastair, "and we never see you or him again. If you do love him, keep him away from us."

Paul wished to ask what sort of state, precisely, Bertie was in, but it did not seem wise to interject.

"Is that a threat?" If anything, Lucas sounded amused.

"I can't overstate how much of one." Rather than amused or playful, Alastair was tired; Paul knew it as surely as he knew Molly would be downstairs readying things for tonight's customers. He judged by the dimming light that it was late afternoon, or perhaps nearly time for an evening meal. "Unlike him, I actually know how to make bodies disappear."

He should have been more disturbed by the statement, but it only made him feel safer.

"He would have been caught." Lucas spoke with clear, soft agreement. Knowing this was about his body and its disposal, Paul still kept quiet.

He understood that any ensuing tumult was not what Lucas would have wanted for the subject of his affections. However short lived it might be for someone with money. He imagined that the rich could possibly explain things away in a manner that was inaccessible to the poor, but he was not optimistic enough to assume all suspicion or liability could be swept away unless one was a peer or aristocrat.

Even then, there were scandals and lost reputations. Whatever Bertie might have suffered should he be successful in murder but caught out by poor planning, Lucas did not want him to suffer at all.

"And a crime of passion would hold no water," said Alastair. "We're not in France."

When he came away from the window, the floor creaked under Lucas's feet. "I have no idea what life will look like, but I can promise you won't see either of us again." There was a note of apology, but Paul knew he would not receive a proper one.

"I don't care what your life looks like," said Alastair. "I don't care what you do, as long as it isn't here. I hope he sells the fucking house, too, because it isn't nearly far enough away from us. We're practically neighbors if he stays."

"And James won't see us, either. Neither him nor his father, that baker," said Lucas.

"I should hope not. They had nothing to do with this."

With another smile that was only a ghost of the thing, Lucas said, "Farewell, you bastard."

Then he quit the room without anything more said, which was just was well. Paul did not want a goodbye, though he could not care less about seeing Lucas again. He wanted only to stop sitting upright and to sleep off the last few days.

Besides, his instincts told him he wouldn't be troubled by Lucas and, though he could not understand them, whatever feelings Lucas held for Bertie were genuine and deep.

They would be his compass now, not petty jealousy instigated by a former compatriot who'd only ever done a good deed or two more than Lucas had managed, or ambiguous longing for a man he felt would never be his.

Paul was not sure if he believed goodness should be rewarded, or that men caused their luck. To think so seemed almost cruel, like playing God. But he at last felt some proper sympathy for the likes of Will Lucas, and maybe even for Bertie Calder. As though it could sense his contemplative mood, the canary, which had been lingering silently on top of the wardrobe like a little feathered sentinel, chittered quietly.

Lucas felt it would be an adjustment to see Bertie so subdued.

Like a wraith looking out over the lands of its former life, Bertie lingered by the very window Lucas had used to break in, gazing at the lawn in the direction of the duckpond.

Lucas said to his back, "I'm sure you can have anything you want sent up. Sell the house at your leisure."

"I have little concern for my things," said Bertie, his voice soft, "maybe because most of what's here isn't even mine."

"Everything here is yours, including me." It was, however, something of a true statement that the house and all its contents were more the province of other Calders and not Bertie himself.

"It wasn't always mine, and neither were you." If Lucas

wasn't just hoping it was there, he thought there might be a smile in the last three words.

"Well, I won't lie and say I was always yours, but I reckon some part of me was from the time you unlocked that door for me. Noticed my fucking shoes."

The longcase clock's tick-tock punctuated the quiet, and Lucas thought about how strange yet affirming it was that Bertie was not fighting Alastair's wishes. He had explained to Bertie the need to go—and there was little emphasis required on the need. He was impressed by Alastair's long temper but knew better than to trust it would hold, particularly where Mr. Apollyon was concerned.

"Did you tell them?"

"Did I tell them what?" For a moment, Lucas believed Bertie meant about the more romantic and carnal elements of their relationship. "I do hate to say, but the likes of *them* can see what we are to each other. I didn't need to tell them."

"No." Bertie was still facing the window. Lucas didn't know if he could or should ask that he turn around, and decided to leave him as he was. "About me."

Then, Lucas understood. He wanted to know if his abilities had been divulged. "No. Didn't seem my truth to tell."

And that was the short of it: he actually suspected that, of anybody in the world, Alastair Gow and Paul Apollyon would have believed him. In their short acquaintance, Paul had always felt uncanny, and he'd referenced witchy family. Alastair had long been enamored of darker tales, so much so that Lucas wouldn't be at all surprised to find out he'd somehow collided with a real witch. If Alastair ever sought him out again, or asked about Bertie, he might say. For now, however, it did not necessarily need saying.

It seemed his words motivated Bertie to face him, backlit by cloud-fettered, afternoon sun that lent him an ethereal air. "Thank you."

"And I didn't say you, ah, helped your brother along, either."

"Thank you. But that Apollyon fellow..." Bertie's eyes wavered from his own as he quieted.

Lucas prompted, "What about him?"

"I do not half-wonder if he does what I do."

"You wonder if he sees the future?" He wanted to be more stunned by the question he asked.

All he could manage was mild amusement that he asked it just as one made queries about a sandwich, or hailed a cab. For once Bertie had said it, then explained it, he found that he could not doubt it the more he tried to make sense of things. Not only because of trust—he didn't necessarily trust Bertie with everything, nor could he trust anyone so deeply. But because, unfortunately, he loved Bertie and one of the best ways he could show it was by taking him at his word when it had to do with his own internal life.

Bertie could have done with such a thing well before now. It was little wonder he had gone mad.

"Yes," said Bertie, and the sheen in his blue eyes grew more thoughtful than vexed. "He felt...familiar. Once I got close enough to him to sense it."

The implication given in the words was more than feeling at home with someone in that way a stranger might feel like a fast friend. But Lucas was ready to assume a man who could see the future might be able to recognize another who could do the same thing.

*Wouldn't be any different from hostlers recognizing other*

*hostlers. Or somebody like me recognizing someone like Alastair.* He wondered what the equivalent to a certain type of gait, or an array of telling calluses, or a damning scar, might be for people who prophesized.

In addition, there was nothing to contradict what Bertie said about his abilities. Lucas would go over everything prior to now that might indicate his lover—his headache—was a seer. But that had to come later, as did much else. At present, he felt himself taking on a new role, one of a protector.

"I can't say I know what you mean, but to believe you, I don't have to know."

Gratitude blooming on Bertie's face was his reward, visible in the almost-smile. "So... Alastair has demanded we leave."

"And we should go."

"I don't blame him for putting his foot down," said Bertie.

With a huff—for Lucas was trying to ignore the gnawing question of where he really stood in Bertie's heart, of how long it would take Alastair not to overshadow him, if ever the latter would happen—he said, "Very magnanimous of you, since all this is your fault."

He would protect Bertie, maybe even from his own mind if possible, but never would Lucas allow himself to be too kneecapped by doubt. If they were to move forward, the only way to do so would be without second guessing. Or, in Bertie's case, without obsessing.

It might be too much to ask that a brush with madness would show Bertie he had little choice but to embody at least some of what he was, else he would be eaten by its repression and his own disavowal. But only time would reveal the answer, and Lucas had no intent of abandoning him to the shadows.

Without being unnerved about the realization, he prepared to move forward into whatever would meet him next. He might not have Bertie forever, but he had at least acknowledged whatever fledgling thing was between them, and that felt like enough to start with.

**17**

———

November had arrived and brought with it much cooler mornings, though Alastair was of the opinion that The Queen Anne was even more welcoming when it wasn't warm outside. He had nothing against the high season, but something about the premises seemed to suit autumn and winter more than spring and summer.

He stoked the fire in the landlord's flat's parlor, then glanced at Paul. "Don't you dare get up."

"It's a cold, not a death sentence."

"Of course not, but most people who have colds haven't also almost drowned recently." He frowned; it might not be a cold so much as Paul's body protesting that it had ingested too much pond water. They could not quite tell, although Dr. Jones assured Paul his symptoms were nothing to worry about *if* he rested and took care of his person. It was ideal, as well, that Alastair had not seemed to catch the cold Paul had.

Alastair knew, much as any of Paul's friends and regular customers also knew, he was not terribly capable of either resting properly or taking care of his person. It was, in some ways, the landlord's lot, but Paul was not alone in his work and responsibilities.

Benson lingered down in the taproom, serving alcohol with Alastair's express permission and Paul's feigned ignorance, while Miss Garland and Molly, along with the cook, were seeing to the general proceedings. Molly usually went home this time of night. But it seemed that after Paul had gone missing and she had overheard Alastair falter at the thought of him missing forever, she was more likely to stay and try to be useful in some manner. Gone, too, was most of her reticence around not only Alastair, but also more of the customers.

"You are never going to let me take so much as the smallest walk by myself again, are you?" Speaking from his bundle of blankets on the sofa, Paul smiled.

"Give me about a decade. Then I might." Alastair joined him carefully, easing himself next to Paul without sitting on a foot or a limb. Such was the bundle that it was difficult to judge where all of him was positioned, and Alma might be under the blankets somewhere.

After a sigh, Paul said, "Why do you think he went so mad?"

"Bertie?"

Paul nodded.

Irresistibly, Alastair reflected on what Lucas had said—or not said—about shadows plaguing Bertie, and his seemingly redoubled issues with talking in his sleep. Now knowing what he did about Paul, about Benson, and what he did *not* know, but might be able to infer about anything preternatural around him—should he give it some thought—he might say Bertie's downfall seemed related to magic.

But that could not be entirely correct.

The man had been so dismissed and repressed his entire life that to call the effects preternatural felt, in itself, dismissive. It diminished his awful decisions ranging from the petty to the downright violent. Bertie had to carry some responsibility for what he was, though Alastair was also willing to concede circumstance and fate had likely tempered him into what he became.

It was easier to think clearly about things now Paul was breathing and whole next to him. Far simpler to reconcile with what he knew of Bertie, which was merely that banal pitilessness had shaped so much of him it was a wonder he'd ever managed to strike out on his own. Continued to connect with Lucas under his brother's, if not his parents', noses.

"I think," Alastair said, "there are things that happen to us in childhood, perhaps, that taint us, and if we're not careful, they can become more poison than anything."

"Lucas didn't have a wonderful time as a boy, I wager. And he wasn't the one who sedated me, tied me up, and threw me in a pond. Must be more than that alone."

Some were brutal from birth, it seemed, and in Alastair's long study of the criminal element, he knew humanity was capable of callousness without there needing to be any kind of reason why. Still, he did not think Bertie was one such person. Old Ross had been, as evidenced by Lucas's reluctance to speak about him at all. He'd seemed to delight in cruelty.

Yet Paul was right, and Lucas had not absconded with him. As the flames settled into the log Alastair had just added to the fire, he said, "When you met him, did you notice anything strange about him?" He was curious and didn't plan on mentioning what Benson had initially remarked.

"Other than how close he stood to me?"

Alastair had to smile at his mulishness. "I mean, the colors you sometimes see, the...like how you say mine are different shades of green. The smells."

Wriggling, Paul shifted so he could look Alastair in the eye. "You mean, do I think he's a witch?" In truth, he sounded annoyed. "Not everyone has a color, for me, and if I am to be completely honest, I'd been so furious that he kept trying to get me to leave you—"

"He wanted me to leave you. He'd have been pleased for you to stay here."

Unimpressed, Paul carried on. "He seemed volatile, but oddly familiar. I don't know why. The accent, I suppose, played a part in any familiarity. He sounded more like he came from Norfolk when he spoke to me, I would imagine." Alastair took volatile to mean in the normal, natural fashion, with which he would agree. "As to the rest, rotten colors. Like bruised fruit finally gone off. I don't think he was happy, not at all."

As much as Alastair might want something preternatural to account for Bertie's singular focus upon him, he could not say with any true conviction that it did. Of course, he had read of Cassandra, who had gone mad, but that had been quite a different situation from romantic obsession. It hadn't been her abilities themselves that posed the most trouble; it was the disbelief of those around her.

*Well, perhaps there is a similarity there.*

Instead of disbelief, though, it would have to be the

dismissal of those around him, or an inability to fit anywhere for fear of exposure. The thought of Bertie having some kind of magic still nagged at him, particularly since Paul said he felt familiar. But deciding if Bertie had any preternatural powers was simply not relevant as this present moment. Indeed, he had no desire to devote this much thought to Mr. Albert Calder ever again. He'd read sincerity in Lucas's eyes and tried to trust he would keep Bertie well away.

"Why do you ask?" Paul kissed his cheek.

"No particular reason." It was the lightest of lies, the smallest of lies. Unlike many of the sins of omission and evasion he had committed, some recently, it was an outright falsehood and would be confined to this moment. In the end, it did not matter what Bertie was or wasn't, or what personal demons he might be battling. "I suppose you don't need to be under the influence of magic, or have it, to do bad things. I never was."

"You never did anything like what he did to me."

"Not without reason." On that subject, Alastair would no longer omit or evade. Paul understood the shape of things when it came to his past, and Alastair finally wanted him to see more because he no longer feared being dismissed or left alone. "Material reason, I mean to say. He felt he had his reasons, I'm sure."

"I knew you would come."

"You had a vision about it, or you hoped I would come?"

"Hoped, if you want to put it that way, or I trusted you would."

"I'm glad Lucas finally showed a conscience."

"Love makes us do strange things, especially when we

think our beloved might ruin our chances before we've even begun."

---

BERTIE MADE his way to The Queen Anne once more, this time well after the public house had been open. It was difficult because Lucas was keeping such a watch on him, and though Bertie had said he was not in any danger of harming himself—or others—Lucas did not appear to integrate the assertion. Only after he had fallen asleep this evening, before bedtime and in a chair opposite the parlor's fire, was Bertie able to make his way into town.

He had walked, figuring the fresh air would do him some good and if Lucas wished to catch up to him, likely able to divine where he had gone, he could do so.

It did seem Lucas was actually sleeping. Bertie arrived at the pub alone, chilled and slightly more clearheaded than usual. As if a fog had been lifted, he went inside with the intention of offering some type of closure rather than simply disappearing as Alastair had done years before. He did not think he could deliver an apology; they were foreign to him.

Father had told Michael often enough that Calders did not say sorry. Although such advice had never been said directly to him, he had both overheard it and been the recipient of its effects. Michael would've died before saying sorry to him, not that he'd ever voiced or intimated the required remorse.

Unfortunately, Bertie was a Calder, too.

The taproom was passably busy with the air of place whose regulars had started to trickle home for the night. He could not see Mr. Apollyon, and was relieved by it, but Alastair spotted him with a bird of prey's quickness. He was not behind the bar, which was being tended by the same creature who'd been inside the first time Bertie paid a visit.

Cutting short a conversation between himself and two others appearing to be fishermen, he made his way over. "I told Lucas I didn't want to see you again."

"He doesn't know I'm here," said Bertie, meeting his eyes with an irresistible, small measure of shame. He did not know if he could act upon it or what that would do, but he was unsettled to note it was there. Generally, he did not associate any of his interactions with Alastair with shame, though he also knew it was not present because of their past liaisons.

It was present because of what *he* had done. All the same, it was not easy for Bertie to imagine himself delivering an apology; he could not even begin to say if he was sorry for what he had tried to do. But that the shame was there had to signify something good about his character. He hadn't thought he had much goodness in him, now.

"If you're going to try making an apology, I don't want one," Alastair said, and he began moving them to one side, a less crowded corner by the bar, not touching Bertie at all, yet starting to walk in such a way that Bertie had little choice but to follow to continue speaking with him.

That made things simpler. "My boy, I don't—"

"Stop. Don't call me that."

"Right." Bertie supposed he would not have long to think about breaking the habit. It was almost painfully clear how much Alastair did not wish to see him—of course, he had said so, but the taut set of his face did not conceal his fury.

Counting himself lucky that they were around so many people, for Alastair seemed poised to hit him, Bertie said, "I only wanted you to know I was, indeed, going."

"Why?"

Lifting a shoulder, because he could hardly explain why to himself, he replied as simply as possible, "I should like to make some different choices in the future, and be more..." a few words would fit. Considerate, equitable, gracious.

"Less yourself," Alastair supplied, about to say more, none of it kind by the look in his dark eyes.

"I *told you* he had some magic." The man who looked like a ragpicker tending bar had shuffled over, silently, and spoke from nearby the shelves of liquor. His torso was bent over the partition that separated barkeep or landlord from customers. He nearly cackled with glee. "I don't know what sort, since his colors have gone all rotten, but it's there. I didn't see them, last time, but then, my eyes weren't open."

Bertie froze where he stood, glancing at Alastair to see if he even humored the words.

Surprisingly, he seemed to, shaking his head in some resignation and looking, briefly, at one of the crossbeams above their heads as though asking a saint for patience. "Don't you start, Benson," he said to the ragpicker. Then, he switched his gaze to Bertie, and it contained minutely less fury compared to a moment ago. "He is generally correct about these things, though."

"An old madman?" Bertie could not prevent himself from defaulting to bluster.

"Better an old madman than a spoiled, lost brat."

"You had best respect me," snapped Bertie. "Or mind yourself."

"Bertie." Alastair did not raise his voice, but it was infused with warning.

"I have been called far worse," Benson said, for all the world a little smug that *he* was not being reprimanded.

Bertie wanted to hit him. "I should think so," he muttered, straightening his bowler.

Huffing, Alastair nodded toward a door Bertie had not yet gone through. Buildings like this, older ones, might have any manner of quirks and partitions added over the years. He had not considered The Queen Anne might be of an age with his own home, but the way the taproom was arranged belied how old it was. Bertie would guess it had been built sometime in the last century.

"Come," Alastair said, and Bertie imagined they each shared the same level of resignation. "Nobody would care if they overheard anything we said, not here, but it's a bit loud." He seemed to consider saying something more. "And I want Paul around for this, too."

The last person Bertie wanted to see was the man he had almost killed by drowning, even if they shared any kind of ability. "Why?" If Mr. Apollyon did, it struck Bertie as rather funny that *his* visions also had not warned him of anything substantial or perilous coming to him.

Alastair did not answer him.

"May I come?" asked Benson.

Bertie wanted to say no, directly, but recognized it was not his place. He hoped Alastair would say it.

He almost did. "Who would serve, if you do?"

"Fair point." Benson looked at the little throng. "Miss Garland has gone home." He looked around at Bertie. "You, sir, are causing yourself a world of trouble. And you cannot keep dragging men into duckponds because of it."

Alastair intercepted Bertie by the arm before he could make a sour reply, and pulled him through the doorway, which led to an entryway that featured a handsome, if worn, flight of stairs, along with an alcove housing a desk, and what appeared to be a small common area just near the stairwell. The front door was obscured by the same vestibule Bertie had noticed on his first visit.

Despite his dislike for Mr. Apollyon, even Bertie had to admit the effect was cozy and almost dignified, save for the worn and eclectic nature of the furnishings. The light was low and presently furnished by candles.

"Wait here," said Alastair, in a tone that would brook no objections, and he went up the stairs without waiting to hear an acknowledgement of the command. Supposing *here* meant the little, demarcated common area, Bertie settled on a narrow wingback chair upholstered with faded brocade. He did not sit all the way back, far too nervous to relax.

What was it about Mr. Apollyon that meant he had to be here for a discussion of Bertie's most intimate secret? Exempting, of course, Michael, which he knew about anyway. One said quite frank things when one was in the middle of a killing.

Bertie had told Lucas how Mr. Apollyon felt familiar, and he did wonder if there were reasons for it. But it was so new to him to think of his abilities in relation to others; he did not know if he had the courage to tell the truth even in this instance. By the time Alastair's footsteps returned, accompanied by a lighter set of them, he had decided how he would proceed.

Mr. Apollyon might well be able to see the future, too, but that did not mean Bertie had to admit he did. He could admit to a certain affinity—or magic, as that Benson had called it—and leave it at that.

Mr. Apollyon could draw his own conclusions. It would not matter; Bertie would be well away in Scotland soon after he did.

"Here we are," said Alastair, his long strides preceding Mr. Apollyon's to Bertie in his chair, and he stood not unlike a sentinel between the two.

"How dreadful to see you here," said Mr. Apollyon. Bertie silently admitted he deserved it. "I'm told you have magic." He paused, but added, "Whatever kind you do have, I should tell you, I think you need to look after it."

"Yes." Admitting it was not the same as explaining things. "And...you have it." The flat statement was not quite a question, because Bertie was not asking. The same sense of the familiar rested between them, as it had before. Did he recognize it, as well? Otherwise, he had little in common besides the man who partially obstructed Mr. Apollyon from view.

"I do." And that was that; as much as he did not want to provide details to Mr. Apollyon, Mr. Apollyon apparently did not want to provide any to him. In truth, there was probably no other way to behave in their situation.

As though the words had a life of their own, Bertie said without thinking, more to Alastair than Mr. Apollyon, "Is that what he meant by saying my colors had gone rotten? That I've...festered?"

It would help account for his increasingly erratic thoughts, as though he had reached a point in life when he could no longer hide his abilities *and* refuse to acknowledge how his brother's abuses had impacted his life, while *also* neglecting to love as he loved.

Bertie, who struggled with appearing weak, was not comfortable with this line of reasoning, but it rang true. His relentless fascination with Alastair had been a symptom of duress, less the cause of it.

Alastair, not Mr. Apollyon, answered him. "Yes." Bertie knew Alastair wanted to minimize whatever interactions he had with Mr. Apollyon. However, he did not need to worry. The entire visit was not behaving in any expected manner, and Bertie did not want to overstay his welcome, such as it was.

Mr. Apollyon, who had not taken a seat and had ghastly shadows under his eyes, said, "I imagine you've never embraced it."

Bertie smiled without any friendliness. "I hid it."

"Same thing."

Instead of addressing whether or not that was so, because he did disagree and saw no need to discuss it with a public house landlord, Bertie tilted his head to look up at Alastair. "And you?"

"And me, what?"

"Do you have any?"

"No," said Alastair, without any elaboration. "But one could say I've grown quite intimate with it."

Sighing, Bertie tapped his foot upon the worn, but clean, floor. His boot's impeccable, deep brown leather was so incongruous against the old wood planks. "I wasn't well." This, even to his ears, was a comical understatement. "For a while. I believe I was keeping too tight a hand on all I was. Am." Compelled to elaborate even though he did not wish to, he said, "Even now, so quickly after I..." he glanced at Mr. Apollyon. "Snapped, and took you...I feel less out of control."

This was not purely because he had lashed out and it had relieved some pressure, and he would try to do a similar thing again. He wouldn't. It was more as though, having done something so extreme and wicked—which some part of him did not want to do—he could now choose to do better. He did not expect Mr. Apollyon to give him much understanding. It merely felt necessary to say he felt more lucid.

"For the sake of others," Mr. Apollyon said, "I'm happy to hear it."

He asked himself whether Lucas would help him stop hiding, or stop giving into erratic behavior. *He already has.*

He nearly wished he could be the sort of man who would talk of magic with another who had it, too, but he was not. He might never be. Perhaps he could grow to accept it better, and supposed he needed to be content with that possibility alone.

"Bertie." Alastair gazed at him.

Bertie wanted to recall the way the candlelight flickered in his eyes, so he stared. "What?"

"Go home." This was said without bile, but it was still like a door closing with someone to secure the lock behind it. "And then go away."

---

THE DECISION CAME to Alastair like it had been delivered by a deity, or with the swiftness he imagined Paul felt when he had a premonition, or that which Benson had experienced when a ghost appeared in his only mirror. Paranoia might have been dictating his actions. But, despite Bertie's recent and uncharacteristic contriteness, he felt Bertie might never actually leave him alone.

Trust had to be rebuilt, after all, and earning Alastair's trust was difficult unless one happened to be a landlord with captivating hazel eyes and a convenient cellar.

It took very little time to act upon his decision, too, and so Alastair found himself in Edinburgh one cold, early November night with a precise and illegal goal. The excuse given to Paul, and Miss Garland, and Benson, was that he needed to tend to something he could only do in person. It wasn't an explicit lie. He just let them all think it had something to do with the landlord of the house he still rented for James, or a bank, or any of the clerical things he knew they thought about.

Benson had eyed him differently, but that was to be expected. And Paul might know or suspect what he had in mind, but he seemed too exhausted to pass any comments. In some respects, Alastair appreciated Paul's trust all the more now, when he was thinking something so drastic.

Alastair had decided he was going to kill Bertie, so he went back north with that express purpose, moving like a ghost or an angel of death. After watching through the windows to make sure, it was clear that the Calders' house still belonged to Bertie. To both his amusement and faint regret, Lucas was also in residence, though he had seemed to leave for the evening on the night Alastair watched them.

He wondered how Lucas's presence might be explained to the neighbors, but supposed it either didn't come up or could be rationalized with whatever reasons Bertie cared to give. As long as the nature of their association wasn't too obvious, it might go unnoticed for years.

That gave Alastair pause. Perhaps Bertie had changed, just as he had himself. In the end, however, he did not know if he trusted Lucas to keep Bertie to heel, or for Bertie to have changed at all, and the last thing he wanted was for recent events to repeat in Cromer.

Paul was at stake, and he was more important than somebody else's liberty, healing, or newfound love, no matter that Alastair wanted to be the sort of man who believed those things were just as valid as his beloved's safety. He couldn't. On the same night he had arrived and spent an hour watching for lights in the windows, confirming Bertie was there and discovering Lucas was, too, he slipped inside through the servants' door and padded through the dark and quiet house.

No servants were in residence, which he imagined was a change for Bertie, but they would probably still come in the morning.

He knew how he was going to accomplish his task. Smothering him would do. It could be proven as foul play, but he would be long gone by the time the conclusion was reached. Lucas would know who did it, and perhaps he would come south as Alastair had gone north. Alastair would contend with that if it happened.

"Did you think I had gone?" Lucas spoke from the shadows of the landing just as Alastair mounted the last stair below it.

Alastair did not so much as jump. "I should have expected you wouldn't have, if you love him so much." It was true, and his pride was not insulted at being apprehended.

"I do, Christ help me, not that I quite know what it means or why I've chosen now to act on it. Known him years."

"Love isn't very biddable, I've found." Alastair sighed. There was nothing like dire events to bring men together, too. "Are we going to fight? I haven't a gun, just knives."

"No, we're not."

"What are we doing, then? He's a rabid dog, and I don't trust him."

Lucas shook his head slowly. "He's not. He'll recover. I can see him changing, even now."

"If I had tried to drown him, you would be doing the same thing to me." Taken aback, Alastair just watched as Lucas came closer to him, not with an air of one who wanted to do violence, but with an air of docility and even supplication.

"I think he will be as he was when we met him. When *I* met him. I think he will be better than that. It might take time, but he can get there."

"Never heard you sound hopeful before," said Alastair, looking down several inches at him, and studying his expression for any duplicity. "I'm not sure I like it."

"I don't know if I do, either. I should just let you do what you came to do. It would be simpler. But I can't." Wan and deferential, Lucas put a hand on Alastair's chest as though to stay him. "Just let us be. If he gets worse again, I'll see to it he doesn't bother you or your Mr. Apollyon."

He had questions he wanted to be answered, and doubted they would be to anything resembling the concept of satisfaction. Lucas spoke as though he knew why Bertie was unwell, or why he was on the mend. That reason could have been his removal to a place well away from Alastair and Paul, but there was so much on the edges of Alastair's knowledge that he knew the change of scenery was not everything.

"Did he ever actually love me, do you think?" Alastair had to ask. He did not want Bertie to have actually loved him, but he did want to know what Lucas thought on the subject. "Or was I what he decided to accrue like a toy?"

Lucas paused before he answered, tonguing his lower lip. For once, Alastair did not mean to wound him, and he did not seem to take the questions poorly. "So much of it is his to tell, but I will say, something caused him to lose his grasp on what's real, what isn't...and I think you were caught in the crosshairs." Motioning him down the stairs from where he'd come up, Lucas added, "Come, I don't think we'll wake him, but I can walk you out."

"Walk me out?" Alastair echoed it with dark amusement.

"It's too strange being in this house as a guest, sometimes. Rather talk in the garden if we have to talk."

"I'm not sure I need to talk much more."

"I do, a little. And this damn house is haunted, I swear. Keep hearing footsteps and whispers in empty rooms. Seems like a friendly enough ghost, but I'm not used to it."

Alastair concealed his amusement at Lucas' skittishness. "Fine." He let Lucas lead him the short way outside, this time through the front door and directly in front of the house. A nearby streetlamp gave them enough light to see by. When they had stopped walking, he said, "If he fucks up again, I don't care how much you love him."

"He won't."

"I fail to see how you can promise that."

"There won't be any more demented valentines coming your way, neither crows nor notes nor rumors."

A light rain had been falling since Alastair arrived, and it both chilled and calmed him. The scent was something so familiar he could not help but relax a little, despite both the errand and the topic at hand being of a more distressing nature. He drew a breath, released it, and said, "If you love him, keep him away."

"Understood," said Lucas. There was no rancor that Alastair could detect.

"You're certain you understand?"

"Perfectly. And it isn't as though he and I began as a wonderful little fairy tale."

Had he and Lucas been real friends, Alastair might have pointed out that so many of the fairy tales started darkly. He did not. Almost all of them did, and not all of them ended in the light. He often wondered how his and Paul's would conclude, but he had no way of peering through the veil to see and even if he could, there was no promise that what he saw would hold truth.

"Bertie has certain…abilities." Lucas peered at him, obviously hesitating to say more, and if he were speaking to somebody else, that somebody might well call him mad.

But now that Bertie had owned to it, Alastair knew what Lucas might mean. "Well, what are they? Does fire come from his fingers? Can he see ghosts?"

Lucas's guarded expression belied a little shock, then resignation.

"The future?" Alastair pressed.

Naturally, given his sense of decorum and added resentment for Paul, Bertie had not confirmed any details of what he could do. But Alastair had been in The Queen Anne long enough that he could make reasonable guesses.

The resignation melted into wide eyes and a slightly open

mouth. Lucas sighed. "How the fuck could you have guessed that?"

"Never mind how." Alastair was too busy thinking back to Bertie's odd way of talking in his sleep, now concluding it really had been indicative of the same kind of thing his own seer would do. He was bone tired, so it might be that shock would show itself later, as his emotions often did after an initial reaction.

But he could not even decide what, or if, he would tell Paul of Bertie's specific talent.

It felt worse for the similarity to exist at all, and he did not know how Paul would react to knowing they were each prone to the same kind of witchery.

He was hardly able to examine what it might say about *him* that he'd been drawn to two people with such an ability.

If Bertie could see the future, or versions of the future, Alastair conjectured that he did not have the fluidity of mind to allow himself any grace. Not with his father being so dogmatic, and not with his own temperament. If one thing about Bertie had usually proven true, it was that he could compartmentalize and disregard better than almost anyone else Alastair had met. After all, he had managed their affair with an efficiency that some only spared their matters of business. Yet that efficiency had masked such violent emotions.

Evidently, his own habits had worsened and infected him with instability. Had there not been the events of the last few weeks to contend with, Alastair might have felt more sympathy. He mulled over what little Bertie had said in The Queen Anne's common area, with scorn and grudgingly, but in earnest.

As things were, his thoughts were drawn mostly to Paul and the unpleasant question of whether he could ever suffer a similar brand of madness that Bertie had fallen into—was it the seer's lot in life? He would remain close even if so, even if it meant seeing Paul's beautiful steadiness erode. Paul, however, had grown up acknowledging and using his preternatural abilities. He embraced them.

Perhaps there was the key.

Blinking, he realized Lucas spoke.

"Mr. Apollyon. He *said* some of his people had been accused of witchcraft." He should have known that Lucas was too intelligent not to draw certain conclusions. "Your fucking husband, or whatever you two call each other...he sees things, too."

Rather than gratify that with a reply, Alastair merely tilted his head in what could have been an affirmative if one sought a yes.

With a muffled sort of laugh, Lucas said, appearing to consider something else, "You *did* know there wasn't anything under that house, didn't you?"

"Yes." That, Alastair would not deny.

"You were far too calm. Not even a flinch." Unsure if he was about to be hit, Alastair took a step back. But Lucas seemed to be thinking too much to want to hit him, his eyes moving and gazing at nothing in particular. "Shit," said Lucas, "I wonder if they had some sort of odd effect on each other, and that was part of what got to Bertie."

"We shall never know. I don't know if that would be everything—Bertie broke before he got to Cromer, and we both know it."

"You're correct about that," Lucas said, and it was loaded

with a wealth of meaning and emotion Alastair did not care to learn. "Although, he's already getting better, now." Few things beyond a love story would have moved him, and although he could not trust with any logical reasoning, he could believe Lucas might change his behavior for love by any definition of the word.

He had done so himself, even before Paul, amending his habits and wishes to marry Evie. That had not been romance, but it had been friendship, and was strong in its way.

He had even changed course to help Muriel and Abigail's love. Before that, Mr. Adair's love for his daughter had proven so prodigious, it had changed Alastair's life. He was a great believer in it, even if he otherwise wished to slap the scarred face that was inches below his own. There was too much history between him and Lucas for him not to, and none of that history would ever be discarded. They each had such stubborn drives for survival.

His, though, had transmuted to a protective urge some time ago. He could detect a similar protectiveness budding in Lucas's countenance now.

He said, at last, "I've had enough of Bertie Calder for a lifetime, but if you want him for yours, I only wish you well."

On an almost shy sort of smile, Lucas said, "I shall guard my seer, and you'll guard yours, it seems."

# EPILOGUE
## CROMER—JANUARY 1873

*"Our life is all grounded and rooted in love, and without love we may not live."*

— MOTHER JULIAN OF NORWICH

In a surprisingly short amount of time, the only story Paul Apollyon cared to tell about Albert Calder or Will Lucas was founded mostly on refraining from saying anything that he thought about any of it. It was a tale shaped by absence. Truthfully, there was no story he *wanted* to tell.

If anything, he wanted to forget it, or at least rarely speak about it. He did not know what there was to say about magic and the preternatural playing their part in driving Bertie mad, or why that madness seemed to alternate between the cruel and the mundane. Maybe he did not like to consider that particular topic due to what it might imply for his own state of mind, given his own preternatural talents.

Alastair had returned from his mysterious trip to Edinburgh and Paul carried on allowing him to think everyone believed he'd merely gone to attend to something to do with James and the bank, or some unfinished thing from his past. In a way, he had been tending to a loose thread, only it was not clerical.

Miss Garland, Benson, and Paul all agreed they thought Alastair might be trying his luck at helping Bertie to an early grave. Paul had spent a few days alone in his flat wondering if it were so. Even Miss Garland, who now knew only the crucial details because she did not care to hear about how Paul had nearly been drowned on his way to her home, quietly agreed it seemed likely. She also said it was romantic, and Paul did suppose it was.

But when Alastair had returned and let himself into the landlord's flat with his extra key, Paul had asked from his seat by the fire, Alma in his lap, "Did you do it?" The small glass of brandy trembled only a little in his grasp as he awaited an answer.

"No," Alastair had replied, knowing precisely what he'd meant by it. "Lucas has him well in hand." They did not discuss the trip any more deeply than that, and actually, Paul was relieved Bertie was still alive. He did not esteem Lucas, but he now trusted Alastair if he said the matter was under control.

He imagined Lucas would take issue with Alastair having killed Bertie, and would make it their problem. He had had enough of men coming from the north and crashing into his establishment. And Bertie's social standing would have complicated a murder, too. Though not an aristocrat, he moved in higher circles where people would notice his absence. Even if the actual chance of Alastair suffering legal punishment might be slim, Paul would rather not think of him coming to harm for murdering the man who'd attempted to drown him.

As romantic as the gesture might have been.

Paul supposed wanting to forget was a natural response to traumatic things. Apart from traumatic, so much of what had happened was clandestine and horrid. For anyone else to begin to understand it, he would have to admit to many dubious things, from the reality of magic, to men who preferred men, to reformed criminals, to a not-entirely fabricated story about someone's long-gone smuggling relatives.

He *wanted* to keep his eyes fixed on his public house and his husband, both of which had undergone certain transformations since last Halloween—just as he had himself. The Queen Anne had been legally renamed to The Shuck, raising a few eyebrows but ultimately going through without issue, and Alastair seemed more unburdened than Paul had ever seen him. That, unlike the rest, felt simple for Paul to understand: there was nothing more Alastair was waiting, or dreading, for Paul to discover about him.

As he watched Alastair traipse through the full taproom with dirty glasses in hand, he smiled, wondering how it was he had ever run the place without him. But it was not The Shuck who had needed help—it was him, for he had not realized exactly how lonely and rather stagnant he was prior to Alastair tearing into his taproom on an otherwise mundane day.

"Are you sure you are all right?" Miss Garland's question forced him to refocus.

He smiled, because he was, though he knew he must

seem abstracted for her to be asking. Either that, or she assumed he was having a vision, which he occasionally forgot she believed in.

"I believe so. I was just thinking about how Laurence was so disgruntled when we changed over the name this month, even though *he* started it in the first place." A lie, but a benign one, and he didn't wish for her to worry overmuch about his head being stuck in autumn when a new year had turned.

Providing a convenient excuse, Laurence was only a few chairs away from the bar at a table full of fishermen who smoked even more than he did, probably grousing about the bad luck bound to follow the young Apollyon now he'd dared to rename his family pub after Old Shuck.

"I believe in a lot," said Miss Garland, with a smirk, "but I cannot be bothered to worry you've cursed yourself just by changing a name."

She accepted her beer with a nod of thanks, leaving an extra bit of money for Paul to have one of his own, and slipped off to join the man who appeared to be her companion for the evening, a slender fellow in a reasonably respectable suit and rounded hat. He let her go, thinking he had only to keep a very mild eye in her direction tonight. Unlike some of her clients, this one seemed well behaved.

As he pulled himself a pint, his mind wandered to the matter of Bertie's empty house, which he had overheard two older, male customers asking Daniel about. They had passed it earlier that day, they said, and did Daniel know if it was vacant again so soon? Both of them were from Cromer, but had moved away and were merely visiting. Paul did not know them, though Daniel seemed to. They were curious about the house's status now. Some of the others had remarked it had been occupied in October and November, but as December drew on, it looked unoccupied again.

The Calders' country house was, so far as anyone still local knew, empty even now in late January. They proclaimed the vacancy a proper waste and wondered where the most recent resident had got to. There hadn't been many employed there during this occupancy—not nearly as many as anyone might assume. But at least one maid and a butler were out of work again.

It had to be said, of course, that there was no accounting for them who had houses like that one. The family had always kept to themselves, it was believed. Some older gossipers said they remembered parents and two boys, and when they were not present, a groundskeeper.

Around Christmas, youths had apparently begun believing it was a haunted place worth visiting for the ghosts, but no authority figures seemed terribly concerned about the issue. It was assumed that no doubt the Calders maintained a watchman. Perhaps the prior groundskeeper's son, or some other relative, kept up the role.

Paul could have told anyone who asked him that there was no such man. That the last remaining Calder was a bit unwell and had been removed to Edinburgh by a friend of the family under strict orders never to return. But nobody asked. That was lucky. He did not know if he could muster such a phrase to refer to Lucas and keep his expression neutral at the same time.

Neither Paul nor Alastair really spoke about last October, though Paul sometimes dreamt of the country house overgrown and empty, silent but for the calls of birds and foxes, still presenting a far grander vision than the empty farmhouse outside Trunch where he had first heard of Albert Calder and his madness for Alastair. They were ordinary dreams. The feverish foretastes of being bound and nearly drowned, and his real recollections of being moments away from being thrown into dark water, had begun to fade.

The visions—only, as it turned out, warnings of a possibility, or maybe a timeline unfulfilled—felt stronger to him than the reality that Bertie had nearly succeeded in drowning his perceived rival. A nobody. A landlord who rarely left his pub.

With good reason, as whenever he left, it seemed his chances of survival dwindled. He knew that was not entirely true. Nonetheless, it might be some time before he chose to venture forth again.

As his warm nightmare of a man came to him smiling, he had a feeling that after closing time, he was about to remember the other reasons why he was not so keen on drifting from home. Unlike many men, he did not have to dream of what those inducements to stay close might be.

# ABOUT THE AUTHOR

Camille is a thalassophile who sadly spent too long residing in Chicago, where there's just a very large lake and no sea. An enquiring and possibly over-educated mind, she's been described as "the politest contrarian." Though everyone believes she's tall, she's not. Likewise, she doesn't dress in all-black.

A small press bound by the belief that every voice matters.

Sign up for our newsletter to learn about new releases and more.
https://oliver-heberbooks.com/subscribe/

Follow us on social media:

facebook.com/oliverheberbooks

instagram.com/oliverheberbooks

amazon.com/oliverheberbooks

youtube.com/@OliverHeberBooksPublisher